WITHDRAWN

Both Sides of the Fence

Both Sides of the Fence

Jean Chapman

ROBERT HALE · LONDON

ISBN 978-0-7090-8890-5

Robert Hale Limited
Clerkenwell House
Clerkenwell Green
London EC1R 0HT

www.halebooks.com

2 4 6 8 10 9 7 5 3 1

Typeset in 11/15pt Sabon
Printed in Great Britain by the MPG Books Group, Bodmin and King's Lynn

PROLOGUE

EVERSING, SHE SAW her peril only at the last moment and braked hard, foot to floor.

She felt the car slew, slide on the soaked ground. Then as she thought it had stopped, it moved again, another metre, backwards, downwards. She slammed the car from reverse to first gear and stalled the engine.

In the dusk and drizzle she had taken the little extra semi-circle of road as an opportunity to do what her Sat Nav said, turn around, and to go back to the last crossroads. She had thought she was travelling alongside a normal grass verge on to open fields, with perhaps a ditch – but the angle of the car was alarming. She sat forwards, gripped the steering wheel, afraid to move more than her head as she slowly turned to look over one shoulder, then with growing terror over the other.

She was poised on the edge of one of Lincolnshire's many waterways. The water lay like dull, flat steel, without a ripple, running to left and right of her, straight and deep through this fenland towards the sea.

She hardly dared breathe as the car hung where it was, angled back but motionless. Her mind made instant recall of the last twenty minutes. There had been a village then a crossroads, where she had obviously gone wrong, mixed up names – Reed St Thomas, Reed St John, St Clements – so many saints. There had been nothing else; the landscape had been flat, bleak, featureless, not a decent-sized tree for miles.

She was, once more, on her own. It had happened before, and she had survived, made the best of things, which was exactly what she was doing now, why she was on this road alone on the edge of night. She was taking the best option life had held out to her – or she had been.

Cautiously she reached to the handle and opened the door, then with a shudder unclipped the forgotten seatbelt. She looked down at black mud beneath the wheels, at the broad track she had scored out of the grassy bank, and saw how close she was to the water.

Without further thought she leapt from the car, then remembering the man who had promised her so much, and who had instructed her to drive from London with his 'most important' belongings, her heart began to pound. She must try to gauge which way would be best to steer to bring the car back on to the road. She had to get this errand right. 'On pain of death,' he had said, but he'd laughed, of course he had.

She must get back in, start the car – she wouldn't close the door – and complete the turn she had started. She wondered if she put the car mats under the wheels this would help.

She slipped on the greasy mud, and half fell into the well of the driver's seat, her ribs hitting the doorsill, taking her breath. She lay for no more than seconds, panting, recovering, and had the mat in her hand when she sensed rather than felt the first quiver, no more than a tremor; it was so slight she thought she had imagined it, though it made her remember her own bag on the back seat. Then there was a positive movement, a smooth but confident slide away from her. She gripped the door. 'No, no, no!' she shouted as if by her will, her desperate need for this not to happen, she could defy gravity, defy the pull of the loaded boot.

She clung to the door, which closed on her shoulder. She span herself round from inside to outside the door, clinging to the edge, but being dragged down with increasing speed to the edge of the water.

She was in the water over her knees when her high-heeled boots hit an underwater ledge. The car responded to the same barrier, wrenching it finally from her fingers, upending it, so the bonnet pointed skywards – and it disappeared like a ship going down in an ocean.

There seemed to be a lot of noise, great eruptions of air from the drowning car, her sobbing, her heart pounding, her protests. Then everywhere was quiet, the silence greater than any she had ever known.

The drizzle had increased, but not heavy enough to be called rain, for it fell silently, collecting and running in drops down her cheeks. She was slipping, her heels sinking deeper into the ledge, the icy water up to her thighs.

It would be so easy to pull her heels free and let herself slide down. At that moment drowning felt like the best solution.

CHAPTER 1

THE BAR OF The Eel Trap public house erupted in a deep-throated roar, which would have done credit to any large male-voice choir.

The shouts of victory from The Trap darts team and its supporters overlaid the groans and exasperation of the defeated. So rarely does the outcome of any match depend on the last man's last arrow, the thrower went immediately into the realms of local history. The following demand for service from the bar was hectic.

Landlord and landlady, both tall, balanced and fit, were approved by many a customer's glance as they filled glasses, passed brimming pints over the counter, went from till to optics, to glass and bottle shelves, fulfilling orders, returning the remarks thrown their way.

The visiting crowd finally made their way to their waiting bus, and with a little encouragement from the landlord, John Cannon, the home team departed in twos and threes. With a sense of weary inevitability he turned to his last customer just as Liz, his partner, was handing over a small parcel. This would be a piece of ham left from the darts supper sandwiches.

'Got the newspaper?' he asked.

The old man flipped his cap on to his head and slapped his pocket. 'Should 'ave asked, should I?'

'Why make tonight an exception? Get off home, or I'll ring up and have 'em do you for being drunk in charge of a bicycle.'

'Aah! You would an' all, bloody London coppers.'

'Depend on it,' he shouted after him and was rewarded by his most faithful customer's cackling laugh.

He stood on the doorstep and stretched his arms skywards. It had been a busy night. He shivered and yawned as he watched the red rear light's wavering pattern as Alan Hoskins began the two-mile ride to his waterside cottage. John had come to know that these regular sniping remarks about his and Liz's past life were tests of his good humour.

He was about to turn back inside, to Liz safe being a landlady instead of a community police sergeant in the Met, when he realized that the rear light was stationary and that he could hear someone shouting.

'Alan,' he said aloud, 'fallen off his bike.' Calling to Liz, he began to run to where the red light was now obviously at ground level. He hoped the old chap hadn't broken anything. He could be aggravating with his endless yarns and habit of saying one thing while meaning exactly the opposite, but he and Liz were both fond of the old Lincolnshire poacher – for that's what he undoubtedly was.

John sprinted, calling out he was coming, but as he got nearer he could hear that Alan was talking, as if to someone else, half comforting, half chiding. Then he saw the figure lying at the side of the road.

'Now then, 'ere's help come,' Alan was saying, and in the meagre light from his bike's front lamp John saw him beckon urgently.

'Looks bad.'

John knelt by the inert figure, put his fingers to a neck which had the marble coldness he had felt so often before, but pressing deeper he felt a faint pulse. 'She's alive, but cold as ice, and wet through.' He pulled off his sweater and wrapped it round her shoulders. Alan handed him his jacket, he took it though he wanted to tell the old man to keep it on.

Then he heard Liz coming, running with a businesslike torch. 'What is it?' she asked, seeing Alan on his feet, but in the next moment was on her knees beside John.

By the brighter light they could see short, stark, blonde hair, and a face so marble-white she looked like a garden statue against her black clothes.

'I can't see any obvious injuries,' John said, 'but she's terribly cold.'

'Carry her back to the pub then,' Liz judged. 'It could take emergency services a while to get out here ...'

'Right.' He stooped, threaded his arms under her knees and shoulders, and as he lifted her he was aware of Liz swinging the light all around the area for signs of what had happened, or where the girl had come from.

'Some heel marks on the verge; looks like she walked from somewhere,' Liz commented. 'And no handbag as far as I can see.'

John registered that the girl was neither heavy nor tall as he carried her as gently and as quickly as he could towards the open pub door. Alan picked up his bike and trundled back after them.

The bar fire was still a mass of red embers and John laid her on the cushions of the long, high settle close to it. The black-clothed figure made a strange contrast to the red cushions and to the lingering atmosphere of two darts teams and their raucous supporters. Liz ran behind the bar and picked up the mobile phone they kept handy under the counter, and repeated the facts succinctly to both the ambulance and police services.

'I don't think she's hurt, good thing she's young or it could be hypothermia we'd be dealing with, but she's been out in the elements long enough. Blankets,' John ordered, and was unbuttoning the girl's coat as he spoke, but seeing Alan come panting into the bar he rose. 'No, I'll get them, you take her wet clothes off.'

Liz grinned at his propriety. She had no doubt old Hoskins had seen it all many times before, but it was such niceties she found endearing in a man the Met had regarded as hard. She took over, registering the fashionable clothes – a black chiffon scarf doubled and pulled through itself inside a black Babrini Koki wool coat, flared boot trousers and high-heeled Jimmy Choo boots – not the kind of gear worn on a cold February night in the middle of fen country – and all soaked through.

'Did everything for my Doreen at the end,' Alan said as he came to help her lift the girl's shoulders and ease off the coat, but as Liz came to the more intimate garments he stood back. John came with blankets and towels, then handed Alan two hot-water bottles. 'Fill them in the kitchen, will you.' He nodded him towards their private living quarters.

They dried and gently chafed the girl's arms and legs, but she made no movement. The hot-water bottles were wrapped in towels and placed near her feet and by her side.

'I'll make up the fire, keep the atmosphere warm,' John said.

'Nothing much more we can do now,' she answered, 'but wait. The police will probably get here before the ambulance.'

'I'll be getting along then,' Alan said, suddenly anxious to be away. 'No telling how long them'll be. Reckon I'll get home.'

'You found her,' John began, but seeing the old man's agitation he added, 'Well, I can tell them as much as you, I guess.'

'They can come and see me tomorrow if they want,' Alan agreed, pulling his jacket on with some difficulty. 'I'll be around.'

'Your jacket's wet through, *and* your shirt,' Liz said.

'I'll drive you home,' John volunteered. 'I can put your bike in the back of the jeep. I'll only be ten minutes at most,' he told Liz.

The three of them stood a moment longer, looking down at the girl, still ashen-faced and motionless under the blankets. Liz began to pick up her clothes, open and peer into the pockets. There were a lot of screwed-up tissues, some small change, a tube of mints.

'Best not handle anything too much,' John said.

'I know,' she said, wondering what Alan had to hide as she saw the two of them out of the front door. She had heard he was a dab hand at trapping anything that ran, flew or swam. Perhaps some of his catches, or even some of his traps, were against the law.

Left on her own she puzzled over the girl; there was something about her that did not quite add up. Liz realized that had it not been for the good clothes she would have taken the girl for – well, someone who could never afford designer labels. There was something in her features – a pinched look, a narrowness of nose. She brought herself up sharply; no one should make such judgements without good reasons.

She drew up a chair and sat by the girl, holding her cold, inert hand beneath the blankets, talking to her, asking her where she had come from, what had happened. She decided it had been the short blonde hair that had first made her doubt the girl fitted her expensive clothes. It was bleached, but that was nothing: no, it was perhaps the condition of the hair. She remembered her London hairdresser, the treatments and massages, and the intoned information from the girl doing the colouring, or the washing, as to what advantages the particular rinse, strengthener, colour extender or gloss enhancer they were using, would bring to madam's hair. The results had always been great as far as she was concerned. This girl's hair certainly had not been given such care.

But there was something else. The nails were full of fen mud, but the red varnish was good, hardly damaged. She gently drew out and straightened the hand that lay in her palm, rubbing it gently, turning it over and back, then peering closer. Something had been written on the back of the girl's hand in biro, but it had been more or less washed away except for odd upwards and downwards loops and a dot which could have been above an 'i'.

Liz put that hand carefully back under the blankets and stood up to lean over and lift out the left hand. No writing on the back of this hand, but there was something else, something she'd registered before, but had not realized was a tattoo. It was skilfully done, shaded in yellows and gold, to give the look of a raised, wide, plain wedding band on the third finger of the left hand. Liz felt disturbed; it seemed a cynical finger decoration, a kind of cheap trick, perhaps on the girl's part, or perhaps on the part of a prospective partner?

As she replaced that hand she thought she sensed resistance, perhaps some return to consciousness, and began talking again. 'Come on, young lady, we want to know who you are.'

But though she watched carefully there was no movement, no rewarding flutter of the eyelids. She wondered what more she could do. The fire was now well stacked and the only thing that was not swaddled in blankets was the girl's head. She went to the kitchen where her coat hung and fetched a bright orange mohair scarf that she wound over the top of the girl's head and under her chin.

Now she could think of nothing more she could do but to talk on, trying to catch at the girl's mind, draw her back to conscious-ness. 'We're wondering where you've come from, where you are supposed to be. Is someone waiting for you?' She asked the ques-tion, like all the others rhetorical in the circumstances, then stopped abruptly as if the girl had responded in some way. But there was no sign, nothing beyond the feeling that her words had not bounced back, but had been taken in, absorbed.

Why on earth should she think such a thing? Did she feel the girl was pretending, playing cat and mouse? Liz went on talking and watching.

'We just want to know you are going to be all right. And that there's no one else out there needing help. Were you in a car? Were there other passengers?'

She stressed the questions, and watched, but the closed eyelids did not flutter, no tear escaped the corner of the eye, there was no emotion, no anxiety – nothing beyond Liz's instinctive feeling that the girl was not as deeply unconscious as she appeared.

Suspicion had been part and parcel of Liz's daily life during her nine years in the Met, and she wondered if she was just making unfounded deductions. There had been no signs of an attack on this girl's body, nothing to say that she had been in any kind of violent assault or accident. Her colour had gone from deathly grey/white to white, but she would have to be a wonderful actress to sustain this motionless pose – or terribly afraid – too terrified even to show she was conscious?

'Oh! God,' she breathed as images of when she herself had feigned death flooded in, as unstoppable as water from a breached dam. She made an effort to control her breathing, counting ten in, ten out, ten in, ten out. She got to her feet and began stacking table mats, reminding herself she was now landlady of The Trap, and if the bar tables were not wiped at night, by morning beer spills set like pools of clear varnish.

But where was John? She needed him here. Ten minutes, he'd said; all it should take to get to Alan's cottage and back. She glanced at the bar clock, nearly midnight, but could not remember what time he had set out.

'Her colour's better.' John said from the doorway, slipping off the belted raincoat he never did up.

Liz started, re-scattering mats across one table.

'I thought you heard me come in.'

'No!' she exclaimed. She felt her own colour rise, wanted to run and beat her fists on his chest, suddenly understanding why mothers smacked lost children when they were restored to their sides.

He had been wearing that same expensive, but then new, coat when she had first seen him, when he had breezed into CID to change into a more streetwise anorak for observation duties. Swashbuckling was always the word that came to her when that mac was swinging from his shoulders.

'I stopped to make sure there was no car anywhere near where Alan found the girl. I had a brief look all around but nothing.'

She wanted to say she had thought he was just taking Alan home, not starting an investigation.

He went to lean over the girl. 'Looks as if she's warming up. Not moved or anything?'

She shook her head.

'No sign of the ambulance yet?'

'They'll have had several calls at once. You know how these things happen.'

'Yes,' she snapped, much too quickly.

'Liz?' he immediately questioned, but she did not look at him. He was on his way across the bar to her when they heard the sound of a siren.

'The ambulance,' he said. 'They'll be coming over the cross-roads.'

She nodded, stood listening to the approaching vehicle, to the increasing engine noise, to the sound of gravel spewing sideways from its wheels as it swept on to the forecourt, and shivered.

He saw and asked, 'Deal with this?'

'Sure,' she murmured.

John had the front door open, waiting, and in seconds the bulk of the two paramedics seemed to fill the bar. Like a well-drilled team with every move rehearsed, they examined, gave oxygen, wrapped her in shiny foil, complimented the owners of The Trap for all they had done, loaded her on a stretcher and whisked her away.

The bar resumed its normal, empty proportions, Liz bent to pick up one of the discarded blankets, but John took her arm. 'The police will be here soon,' he said with the air of there not being much time to pull in all they had to do. In fact, he was not sure whether the vehicle he could hear was still the ambulance going away or the police arriving.

'Liz? What's happened?'

She shook her head, but he took her arms just above the elbows and held her in front of him. Almost as tall as he was, mid-blonde hair tied back in a ponytail, he had thought she was a replica of so many tall, leggy blondes with long hair, until he had taken a longer, deeper look.

'Look at me, Liz,' he ordered, 'and tell me ...'

In the end she lifted her face and he was shocked as he saw eyes swamped with recollection, with a waking version of the nightmare he still occasionally retrieved her from. 'Liz,' he mourned, and folded her tight to him as he did when she slept the terrors.

'It was the girl,' she said. 'I thought she might be just acting, playing ...'

She did not have to say more. Liz had played dead in a sordid, litter-strewn multi-storey car park. He had been observing through powerful binoculars as her cover had been blown by an informer CID would have staked their lives on. Instead, his superiors had staked Liz's.

He had seen her pinned up against a wall and receive an uppercut that would have floored a heavyweight boxer. Then she had been dragged out into the middle of the car park and a 4x4 driven full speed towards her, to run her over, finish her off. She'd had the wit to remain motionless, let them think she was unconscious, then had rolled out of the way at the last minute, and legged it. He had met her in the middle of the intervening street between observation post and multi-storey.

He had spent the next fifteen months tracking down the drug gang they had been watching, painstakingly picking up the pathetic addicts on the streets, threatening the already pressured under-middlemen, watching the next tier up, moving out into suburbia, to the countryside, to the minor manors and estates of drug barons. He had spent hours of his own time researching their finances, found who laundered their money in overseas holiday complexes, strings of casinos, and uniquely in that case, a brotherhood of bookmakers who travelled the race-course circuits, and so given the case its nickname – The Race Case.

Then there had been the enormous satisfaction of finally, finally, pushing the paperwork to its bitter end, convincing even the Crown Prosecution Service, and getting the Race Case into court. When the gang members were convicted, sent down for twenty years, their assets seized, there had been a surprising after-math for Detective Inspector John Cannon.

The evening after the court case, after the threats from the dock, the thunderous looks from the public gallery, at him and at the stalwart jurors, he had realized that he considered his police work was done, finished.

It had been time to move out and on, to retrieve Liz from her hiding place, to help rebuild her life, as the experts had rebuilt her jaw and teeth.

They had sought anonymity and been unmasked by an old man who read any newspapers he could pick up for free and had an amazing memory. Alan Hoskins had taken three days from their arrival at The Trap to remember who John was from the news photographs taken outside the court. Alan's announcement in the bar had made them uneasy, but it had been all right, worked well up to now.

He felt Liz stiffen as they heard another siren, a different wail – the police. 'Don't worry, we'll soon get rid of them. Not much for us to tell really. What about making some coffee?'

She nodded on his shoulder.

'And perhaps a sandwich or two, you know what it can be like on motor patrol – never know when you'll get your next break.'

They both knew it was truth and a ploy, giving her something to do and an excuse to be in the kitchen while she drove the demons away.

When she returned with a plate of cheese and pickle sandwiches and coffee, the details had been given. The older constable asked her a few questions to confirm what John had already told them, the younger man stood impatiently by as the longer-serving man took his time and a sandwich.

'No accidents reports in the area, then?' John asked.

'Not so far.' The senior constable, grey at the temples, shook his head.

'No,' the younger policeman confirmed, then fixing John with a steady stare asked, 'Aren't you the man who resigned from the Metropolitan police – couldn't hack it?'

The older man cleared his throat and asked, 'So you're sure neither of you had seen the girl around before?'

'We're certain,' John said, thinking that if Alan did not know her she was certainly a stranger.

Then John looked at the young man and answered him. 'That's right,' he said. 'I couldn't, as you say, hack it.'

CHAPTER 2

J OHN STEPPED OUTSIDE the back door of The Trap and relocked it. It was barely dawn and he felt a certain guilt leaving Liz in bed, but for the first time in a week she had slept quietly all through the night. And now he just felt the urgent need to stretch himself physically, to be away from this public house for a bit, from the commitment of their names above the door: John McEwan Cannon and Elizabeth Pamela Makepeace licensed to sell beer, wines and spirits.

He set off slowly, from walk to jog, but the pad, pad of his feet, the silence and the limitless expanse of land and sky around him began to relax the strings of tension and he ran faster. He drew in a deep breath; the wind was from the east and he could smell the ocean.

This bad time for Liz had been triggered by the girl, and then reinforced each evening by Alan Hoskins. All week Alan had scanned John's newspaper for news of the girl. Every night he regaled the bar with the story of finding her, of the police inter- viewing him, and how he might have expected to be informed, seeing as he had an interest.

If he then cast a meaningful glance in John's direction there was a stoniness in the landlord's eye which stopped him pursuing his usual banter about police shortcomings. These encounters, which did no more than create an interesting tension for the regulars to observe, had given Liz nights of unsettled sleep and two nights ago the return of the nightmare when she woke choking and fighting with a might two or three times her normal strength.

John clenched his teeth as the power of the memory almost stopped him running, but he made himself go on, counting each footfall. 'One, two, three, four. One, two, three, four …'

He knew the violent dream almost as well as Liz herself. It re-staged the moment after she had been so violently struck in the face, when she lay in the path of the murderous wheels, swallowing her own blood. He had once made a shaky joke about it, saying she certainly did not want to choke to death before they could run her over. They had clung together, laughed and cried together.

He turned to run faster towards the sea. He had come to know this bit of coast as well as it was possible to define the exact lines of sand, salt marsh and mudflat near the great Wash estuary. Here the Rivers Witham, Welland, Nene and Ouse found their way to the sea, and was where man had for centuries contrived to keep and regain land from the North Sea, when much of it lay three metres below the level of a surge tide.

He topped one of the old earth banks and felt the wind cold, cleansing. The vastness of sky over these lowlands, the feeling of limitless space, helped put him and his preoccupations into proportion.

It was here during his first year at The Trap that he had been startled as five Canada geese rose from the nearby lagoon and flew in a V formation just a couple of metres above his head. He had looked up, amazed at their nearness, at their noisy honking, at the way they had appeared to look down at him and seeing his admiration had seemed to stretch out their necks even straighter. It had felt like a royal fly-past. Ever since, he had watched all the birds, particularly the water fowl, with much greater interest. These days he always pushed a pair of very light binoculars into his pocket and his bird books filled a shelf in the pub office.

He walked along the top of the bank and watched the dawn brighten his world, the palette of colours grow from a concentration of deep rose to pink as the sun shot its warm colours along the sea's horizon. But he could see it would not last; by normal getting-up time the clouds would have taken over.

He put the binoculars to his eyes and slowly circled – bright flashes of water, great masses of dramatic cloud, under-lit now by the powerful burning rim of sun, made him stay his breathing to keep the binoculars steady. From the sea he turned slowly to the land, to where colours were warming to the light, to an opalescence of delicate shades, a transient mother-of-pearl sky. He pitied all who still lay in bed. Then he grunted with amusement as he thought that in all probability Alan Hoskins would not be one of them. He'd be about some nefarious undertaking, augmenting his pension.

The thought that Hoskins might well be sharing this early-morning splendour broke the spell of bitterness and alienation he had built up during the week. He had felt a desperate need to get away; now all he wanted was to run back to the pub, to Liz.

He swung his binoculars to complete his circle – and was immediately riveted by a drama of a different kind. In an area of marsh and mere tracks was a long, black shape that for a moment he did not recognize, it was so unexpected at that time, in that place. He steadied the glasses, adjusted the focus, on a low-slung car, its gleam and lines suggested new, expensive. He frowned as he concentrated and brought the object closer. It was near the limit of the binoculars' range, but he saw something move. It was a man standing talking to someone in the car. He concentrated on the figure. There was something familiar about the stance, a little askew, one shoulder dropped, and at this hour of the morning if that wasn't Alan Hoskins then he was a Dutchman.

A second man got out of the car with something in his hand, a map or perhaps a newspaper. For a moment John wondered if

Hoskins was up to his usual trick of cadging a free read. Then the two figures merged. It looked as if the taller, younger, sturdier man had caught the old man by his shirt front and was holding him stretched up tight against himself.

John heard the protest in his own throat, the aggressiveness of the act perfectly obvious even from afar. He wondered how long it would take him to run over there – too long if real violence was intended. Then as suddenly as the two figures had merged they separated, the driver to crumple over the bonnet of his car, and the other making his escape across the marsh – after, he surmised, managing to put a hefty knee in the other's groin. So, it was true what John had been told: Hoskins could look after himself in a tight corner. 'Slippery as the eels he traps' had been one verdict passed over the bar counter.

The driver struggled up and tried to follow, but was soon stumbling, wallowing, trying to pull his feet free of the black ooze he had stumbled into. He went down on his hands and knees. John could read the fright in his urgent backtracking. He leapt back into his car and reversed at speed along the track, then turned right at the first opportunity as if he hoped to head Alan off. John was not worried that he would succeed as he watched the local man reading the ground, expertly striding across the marsh.

So what was all that about? he wondered, but at least Alan would have a new story to tell in the bar.

He jogged home, knowing he would tell Liz, but not quite sure how to pitch the story in view of the disturbed nights – serious, jokey, offhand? He was still wondering when he came in sight of The Trap.

He walked the last hundred metres and approved all he saw. In the spring and summer there would be flowers, lots of flowers, tubs, hanging baskets over the door and under the first-floor windows, perhaps all along the front this year. He would devise a proper watering system. And they still had those plans to turn the stables into self-contained holiday units, when it could be afforded.

He took off his trainers in the back porch and in stockinged feet listened at the bottom of the stairs. He could hear movements; Liz was up and about. He walked through to the beamed bar with its collection of various kinds of traps (everything from eel baskets, mole traps, rat traps to a mantrap), up the three steps to the dining area. Here old prints hung between the wall beams, pictures of men in small rowing boats water-fowling, men supporting guns looking more suited to battleships, with barrel ends splayed like trumpets to spread the shot. John had felt the prints should stay, but Liz found them dour and had begun a cheerful collection of white pottery ducks. Customers had begun to bring the odd one to add to the collection.

He picked up the lunchtime menu – this they invariably went through over breakfast, Liz deciding the items on offer, and John running the new menu off on the office computer and slipping them into their plastic folders. He was on his way to the kitchen when he thought he heard voices upstairs. Must be the radio he thought, though it sounded just like Liz talking to someone.

He went to the bottom of the stairs and saw Liz coming down with a bundle of clothes. He opened his mouth to speak but she shook her head vigorously and indicated he should follow her to the kitchen.

He frowned an enquiry at her. She in turn closed the kitchen door behind her and pointed to the newspaper delivered while he was out.

On the front page of their local weekly was a rather startled image of the girl, under the banner headline, 'Do You Know This Girl?'

'So they've still not found out who she is,' he said.

'No,' Liz whispered, 'but she's here.'

'Here?'

She put her finger to her lips and shook her head as he made as if to run upstairs and interrogate her that very instant. 'She's in the bathroom, I've just found her some clothes.' She held up the bundle. 'I think she's come from the hospital in someone else's outdoor clothes, a nurse or auxiliary who changes at the hospital, and someone six sizes bigger than she is by the look of them.'

'And how's she got here?'

Liz turned the clothes in her arms and revealed a dark outdoor coat. She slipped her hand into the pocket and drew out a bus ticket. 'It's dated this morning,' she told him, 'so I guess she's walked from wherever the bus dropped her off.

'She's obviously out on some kind of limb – all she's said is "Help me", but …' Liz paused significantly as she drew out a bright orange mohair scarf. 'She brought my scarf back, gave it to me as I opened the door.'

'She …' he began with a rush and stopped just as suddenly. The implication of the girl finding her way back and knowing where the scarf had come from, who it belonged to, made the whole episode far more ominous.

'She was pretending when I was alone with her in the bar,' Liz said. 'I just felt it.'

'She's not come back just to return a scarf,' John said. 'You don't purloin someone else's clothes, and presumably money, then do a runner from a hospital to return a scarf.'

'And what was she doing around here in the first place?' Liz added. 'That's what we have to find out.'

'Another odd thing, and involving Alan again …' He went on to tell what he had witnessed on the East Salt Marsh.

'Alan's name is in the newspaper and The Trap is mentioned.'

He shrugged. 'We must let the local lads know the girl's here. They'll be setting up a full-scale search, using up their manpower and resources.'

'If she finds out she'll run again,' Liz said and tapped the front page of the newspaper. 'It must be because of this she's left the hospital. That girl is desperate not to be found, not to be named.'

John remembered the paper in the car driver's hand. Had he shown that newspaper picture to Alan? He felt a frisson of excitement, the feeling he had known many times in the Met when a case suddenly augured complexity, when what was already known and visible was obviously only the tip of a big iceberg. He frowned as he found Liz watching him closely. She raised her eyebrows.

'We do not have a choice,' he stated. 'It is out of our hands.'

'Quite,' she agreed. 'But we could delay a little,' she urged. 'She trusts me. She probably doesn't even realize what her disappearance will mean.'

John did not contradict, this would not be the first time he had dealt with runaways who were so taken with the thought of escape, what they might be leaving behind in the way of turmoil, grief and search parties never entered their heads.

'We can at least talk to her over breakfast,' Liz said.

He watched as she scooped back her hair, deftly flicking it round and into an elasticated band. It always drew his eye and his heart to that new, slightly askew, jawline.

'OK,' he agreed. 'Over breakfast.'

Liz had made coffee and they had hastily sorted the business of the menu before they heard the girl coming down the stairs. She had on a pair of Liz's cropped trousers, full length on her, and a red fleece. John thought she looked worse than when they had seen her off in the ambulance – her face was thinner and paler. He pulled a chair out for her. 'Just in time for breakfast,' he said, neither of them sure whether the drop of head was acquiescence or exhaustion.

'It was good of you to bring my partner's scarf back,' he said quietly. 'Not many people are that honest these days.'

The girl clasped her hands together with a jerky gesture, like someone sick trying to control a chronic shaking. He pushed her coffee mug nearer.

Liz put cereals and bowls on the table, and the smell of thick slices of homemade bread being made into toast filled the kitchen. 'Is there someone we should let know you're safe?' John asked.

She bit into her thumbnail and shook her head, though it looked more shudder than shake.

'Let's eat.' Liz poured cornflakes and without consulting either of the others, sliced bananas on each. 'Everyone feels better after breakfast.'

The girl began slowly, but finished the cereals and ate a round of toast. John was still hungry but did not want to delay matters with cooking.

'We should introduce ourselves,' he said, pushing his plate aside. 'John and Liz.'

The girl looked from one to the other but did not volunteer her name. 'Thank you for …' A gesture indicated the breakfast and then the clothes.

'Do you feel able to tell us what's happened to you, why …'
She shook her head.

'Is there some reason?' He knew this was a daft question – there obviously was a reason – but it did evoke a reply which he did not catch.

'She doesn't know where to start,' Liz repeated, her glance daring him to suggest something as puerile as at the beginning.

'Do you know where you are?' he asked, not willing to be deterred, and very aware of the police search operation that could be needlessly eating into the chief constable's budget at that very moment.

'Sort of,' she whispered.

He went to one of the dresser drawers where they kept a selection of national and local maps. He opened out several before he found a large-scale one of the area.

'This is where you are now.' He pointed where a square indicated the position of The Eel Trap. His finger travelled inland. 'Here's the crossroad beyond the village ...'

He stopped because it was obvious that the map had caught her attention. Her hand came up and hovered, her fingers falling on the edge of the map as she repeated, 'The crossroads.'

'You can see that the four ways go to four different Reeds – St Mary Reed, St Thomas Reed, St John, St Clements. It's very easy for anyone to go wrong there; a lot do.'

'Yes,' she confirmed, and they waited.

'Which one were you heading for?' John asked, as casually as he could.

The fingers trailed towards Reed St Clements and beyond, generally in the direction of the coast.

'You've been this way before? Been to Lincolnshire before?'

She shook her head, but the way she bent over the map convinced him there was something here vital to her.

He dropped the bus ticket on top of the map. 'You came on a bus this morning, then walked to this pub, to return a scarf? Where were you really going?'

'You felt in the coat pocket,' she said, picking up the ticket.

'We really want to help you,' Liz urged. 'We both know what it's like to be in a tight corner, to feel pushed into doing things.'

The girl's expression changed as she looked at the couple and then around the well-equipped pub kitchen. She shook her head. 'I don't think so,' she said, certainty giving her voice a hard and sudden energy.

'You might be surprised,' he said mildly.

'There must be people worrying where you are,' Liz suggested.

'No,' she denied, 'you are wrong there. There's no one.'

'What about work colleagues?'

She gave a bitter laugh and an underlying Cockney accent surfaced. 'Nah! It was all well planned.'

They both watched as without thinking the fingers of her right hand went to the place on her left hand where the ring was tattooed. It was the same unconscious gesture many women make, turning and twisting their wedding or engagement rings when deep in thought.

'That's very unusual,' Liz said, 'a ring tattoo.'

She spread her hand. 'It's a symbol,' she said.

Someone else's words, John thought as he waited for Liz to go on.

'Of something very nice then.'

'Something promised.' The girl covered the illustration, grasping her fingers tightly. 'But ...'

'But?' Liz prompted.

'It's private.' She stopped, looked sharply from one to the other, with sudden aggression. 'You know you two act like coppers, coming in with your questions, one after the other.'

'What does a girl like you know about coppers?' John asked mildly.

'Oh, I know!' she exclaimed and was up on her feet with all the force of an animal springing from a corner. 'I was there when they questioned my brother, chipping in, one after the other, trying to trip him up. Just like you two.'

John lifted his hands as if in surrender. 'Sorry,' he said.

Liz sat down slowly and repeated the apology. The girl turned away, but went only as far as the window and stood looking out at the empty car park.

'Me and my brother,' she began again, reminiscing quietly, 'we lived together. I looked after him when we were left on our own.' She paused and neither of them moved, waiting now for as much, or as little, as she was prepared to tell. 'Ma died when I was sixteen and neither of us remembered our dad. Well, the coppers came to the house, questioned him about some drug ring at his school. Then the next day he saw the police arrive at school and ran off.' She paused, her voice becoming hard and bitter again. 'Got killed by a bus. So I've no time for the police; they've never helped me.'

'Did you not get ...' Liz began.

'Oh! A lot of people talked to me,' she snapped, 'but that didn't bring my brother back, did it, and I still had to make a living, pay the rent. I had to make my own way.'

John wondered if like many another solitary youngster she'd been forced into prostitution. But she was articulate, gave him the impression of being a girl who would work hard, the sort to have several jobs, rather than opt for the shorter hours, if infinitely more dangerous option, of being on the streets.

Watching her at the window, it struck him that she'd become trapped in something she had been totally unprepared for and now had no idea how to deal with. He was not sure how to word his belief that her best option would be to tell the police everything.

The sound of a car travelling at some speed reached them, going inland, going on past the front of the pub and away – they thought – but there was a sudden scream of brakes and a scattering of gravel as it made a sudden and abrupt turn into the pub's car park.

Could this be the police? Coming back to the point where she had originally been found, it would make sense. He saw the girl's back stiffen and she moved to the side of the window so she could see but not be seen.

At the farthest side of the car park was a black, low-slung Porsche. This had to be the car he'd seen on the track near the marshes.

'Do you recognize it?' he asked, finding that the girl was now behind him, breathing fast, one hand knuckled at her mouth.

'No,' she denied, but too quickly, and as the driver's door swung open, she appealed, 'Please don't tell anyone I'm here. I'll tell you everything when he's gone.'

'Go back upstairs,' Liz said. 'But don't walk about – the floors creak.'

John accompanied her to the stairs; halfway up she turned and mouthed 'please' again. He raised a calming hand then went back into the kitchen, leaving the door open so he would see if she tried to slip out the back door. He strode back to the window; he wanted a good look at this driver, and once he was clear of the car he would be out there to question him.

Liz was hanging the outdoor coat under several others and pushing the other clothes into the washing machine. The word conspiracy, conspiracy to pervert the cause of justice came into John's mind. The driver was taking his time getting out of the Porsche, and his door was still open.

'Damnation!' he suddenly shouted. 'The bitch!'

'What?' Liz questioned, bemused, as John leapt from window to door and out of the kitchen. She heard the car driving away, and John cursing in ever more lurid tones.

She found him standing outside the front door of The Trap. 'Unlocked and unbolted our front door – and was halfway across the car park before I saw her! Then she jumps into the car and they're away. We fell for her and her story right enough.'

He strode back into the kitchen, picked up his phone and tapped in the local police number. After some explanation he repeated, 'Yes, the girl from the hospital – returned a scarf belonging to my wife and has been driven off in a car. No, I know nothing more, sorry.' He put the phone down.

'Feel like a blooming idiot,' he said to Liz. 'All I need is for them to send the same young copper who thinks I couldn't hack it – make my day.'

'A man with a Porsche surely has to be the same man who bought her the designer clothes and those boots,' she said, 'but … she was afraid too, no doubt about that.'

Then, ever practical, she set about retrieving the clothes from the washing machine and the coat from the peg on the door, put the bus ticket back in the coat pocket and folded them all ready for the police.

'As somebody on telly used to say, didn't we do well? I wanted to get a look at him, and his shoes. He has to be the bastard who waylaid Hoskins – his shoes'll be covered in mire.'

'You'll have to ask him when he comes in tonight. He'll be able to give you a good description – you know what Alan's like.' She paused and laughed. 'He might even remember the car number.'

CHAPTER 3

THE EVENING'S TRADE at The Eel Trap started in the usual way
in some respects – a couple of villagers came in, drank
leisurely pints but by 7.30 were glancing at Alan's empty seat,
when a third joined them.

'Late tonight, ain't he,' he stated.

John, stacking bottles, still mulling over the interrogation by a
detective sergeant about the girl's arrival and departure, looked
up, but it was the other customers the man was talking to.

'Not like him, not when he's got ...'

John looked up again, this time to intercept a nod in his direction, as if to remind the speaker to watch what he said.

This was fairly unusual. John's experience was that customers
tended to think that the man serving was either deaf, or that the
bar was a kind of soundproof barrier, and they could repeat the
most scandalous gossip, crude funny jokes, crude unfunny jokes,
or intimate details of their love lives, or lack of it, with impunity.

Just after nine the three locals left, looking, John thought, a
little disconsolate.

'No, Alan,' Liz commented.

By 9.30 the bar was full, with the usual crowd calling in for a
drink after the popular watercolour class held in the village hall.
They were a mixed, cheerful bunch, led by their tutor, Paul
Jefferson, a man who after art college had taken a gap decade,
come home to nurse his mother, but now lived alone. He delivered

his lessons interspersed with pieces of his life story and local anec-
dotes of varying degrees of suitability. John really liked the guy;
Liz admired his work and talked of joining his class. A rival in the
telling yarns stakes, Alan Hoskins never seemed well disposed to
the man, and when Paul Jefferson was in the bar Hoskins was
always quieter, watching and glowering from the single pew-like
seat fixed next to the bar.

Coming to the counter, Jefferson nodded at the empty seat.
'Gone early tonight,' he said.

'Not been in.'

Paul Jefferson laughed. 'You sure? Caught sight of the locals
collecting their usual swag when we came in.'

John frowned as he took back a glass and topped it up as the
froth settled.

'Don't tell me you didn't know!' He tapped the side of his nose.
'That's the reason he doesn't care for yours truly.'

John watched him carry the tray of drinks back to his friends
and pupils, and wondered what Paul knew that he didn't. He was
not sure whether he was more worried because the old boy had
not turned up, or that Paul Jefferson thought he had been and
gone, without coming in for a drink.

John made sure he was nearby as Paul and his entourage left,
and without Alan in residence they were the last ones out. He
followed leisurely, out of the front door. The day's events had
soured his usual enjoyment of the bar custom, the noise, the
conviviality, and he now took pleasure in the settling of the night,
the noise of departure, the goodnights, the noises of car engines
retreating in the distance. Some nights he imagined he could sense
the creatures of the night breathing a sigh of relief as they came
into their own.

Tonight Paul Jefferson lingered by his car, waved his last pupil
off with a 'Don't forget your homework'. He was rewarded with
a question and he shouted back, '"An Early Blooming", your own
interpretation.'

'Interesting subject,' John said, going over to him.

'Some of the results'll be more interesting,' he said with a grunt of laughter, 'but I love 'em all, they're a good antidote to the rest of my solitary life. Now, want me to show you what I meant about Hoskins?'

'Show me?' The offer of being shown was a surprise.

Jefferson left his car, and the car park, walked past the front door of The Trap and led the way through the arched gateway to the old stables. The spotlights under the eaves at the front of the pub gave enough light for them to see in the cobbled yard. Jefferson led the way into what had been the old tack room.

'We really need a flashlight in here,' he said. 'Hold on, I'll strike a match.' The match scraped and fizzed, lighting up the proliferation of hooks and nails around the walls, from which one or two antique pieces of harness still hung. 'See here.'

John could see four nails at head height, nails that even in the momentary light of a second match he could see were smooth, the hafts almost shiny with use.

'Now down here.' Jefferson shielded and lowered the match and John bent to where he could see spots of dark colour on the old brick floor. He touched one with his finger and felt the substantial tackiness of recently dripped blood. 'Alan Hoskins has been using this as a dropping-off place for his ill-gotten catches for years, long before you came. Pops his bike inside the yard here, hangs up his offerings of fur, feather or fish, collects his money during the evening, and thanks very much, landlord, for the facility.'

'Well, I'm damned,' John said, wondering how the money changed hands, then thought how often old Hoskins went to the Gents of an evening. He had put it down to an old man's complaint. The cunning old devil – so that was why so many of his fivers were folded in neat, palmable squares. 'But how did you find out?'

'Only because I came to do some sketches of the place just

before you took over; thought you might spoil it all trying to pretty it up. I was in the yard here, sketching the view out through the archway to the road. Hoskins came pushing his bike, his rack bulging with bloody parcels. He didn't see me until he finished hanging his game. He tried to placate me with a goose. I wouldn't have it – didn't want it – but I tried to reassure him that he need not worry, I'd seen nothing that interested me, but he's not been easy with me since.'

'Why tell me now?' he asked.

Jefferson laughed. 'Because you've been casting anxious glances at his seat all evening. You and Liz are obviously fond of the old rogue, so you're not going to turn him in, are you!'

'So what happened tonight?' he asked. 'You say you saw him.'

'As I swung in to the car park I saw three chaps coming out of the stables with their booty, followed by Hoskins, who as I caught him in my lights looked ...'

'Looked?' John prompted.

'Well, pretty apprehensive. When he never came into the bar I presumed he'd had a scare.'

He toyed with the idea of telling Paul what he had seen that morning on the salt marsh, then decided he'd engaged in enough questions and answers for one day, though he felt it an omission after the other man's confidences.

He watched the lights of the last car off his car park with a sense of indebtedness to Paul Jefferson. He had intended to drive over after closing time to make sure Hoskins had not after all fallen foul of the man he had left floundering on the edge of the salt marsh. Now he felt relieved of the obligation. Hoskins had obviously gone straight home.

'But what stopped him coming in for his usual pint?' Liz asked as she heard of Alan's marketing arrangements.

'Perhaps there was a police car hanging around,' he said, dabbling his fingers under the tap beneath the bar to wash away the congealed blood.

Deep in thought, he sorted the wet beer mats on the bar top, binning those that were soaked and would never dry flat again. 'The girl's the catalyst, the pebble thrown into our pond causing the ripples. What was she doing wandering, wet through, in the middle of a February night?'

Liz brought glasses to the counter, collected from ledges and on windowsills behind curtains, clinked them down, and leaned, watching him. 'Do you think she had a row with the man in the Porsche and he threw her into a dyke?'

'Well, we do know she's connected with the Porsche, and if the owner's her boyfriend there's serious money somewhere. While the girl suggested someone being bought and used.'

'I felt sorry for her,' Liz said.

'So did I, until she did a runner,' he said as he watched her perform that miracle of control with her hair. She always made the ponytail to do any clearing or cleaning up, then after the work was finished freed her hair again, tipping her head back and pulling off the band. Gathering in, or freeing, her tresses, had the same switch-on effect on him.

'So what are you thinking?' she asked.

He cleared his throat. 'I thought I might still have a look at Hoskins and his cottage first thing in the morning.'

'Good idea,' she said. 'Now let's finish wiping round and go to bed.'

'Sure,' he said, manipulating his lips as if he had to chew the American version of the word.

She raised her eyebrows and made a pretend grimace while her brain flashed a picture of him swashbuckling in that raincoat.

CHAPTER 4

HE HAD PASSED Alan Hoskins' cottage on many morning runs, and there was never any sign of life. He had, however, never ventured in at the gate before. He thought it was policy to make plenty of noise doing it. He neither wanted to scare the old chap to death nor be on the receiving end of one of his defensive tactics.

He shouted as he opened the small wicket gate opposite the front door, walked the ten yards along the crazy-paved path to where an ancient trellis still kept its place entwined with ropes of thick old clematis stems.

He knocked loudly, several times, muttering, "'Is there anybody there, said the traveller, as he rapped at the ...'" His gaze fell downwards. '... rotting door.'

He stepped back out from under the trellis and looked left and right. There was a narrow border along the house front where even in the dereliction of briars, grass and bindweed, bright blue scillas were already flowering. He guessed it had been the long-dead Mrs Hoskins who had been the gardener, but he revised this idea when he walked round to the back of the house. Here a vegetable plot was already dug, a couple of compost bins stood empty, the contents obviously already put on to the land. Mrs Hoskins had been the flower gardener.

There was a shed at the top of the garden and a lean-to against the back door. A pair of boots, obviously used for the recent digging, stood side by side under the lean-to, on a ledge was an oil can, a puncture outfit and a couple of old spoons. Spots of oil on the ground indicated this was where Alan kept and maintained his bike. It was gone and so presumably was the old poacher, out and about his business before the great and the good rose.

He might have left it at that had he not been curious enough to walk around to the far side of the cottage and find Alan's bike propped against the wall. He put his hand on the leather saddle and confirmed what he had immediately thought. The bike had obviously been out there all night – the leather saddle was wet through.

Now he was alarmed. He ran to the back door, pounded, shouted, then tried the old-fashioned latch. The door was open.

He was reaching for his phone as he went into the kitchen. He took in the regimental array of old-style aluminium saucepans on a shelf, the black lids hanging on nails beneath them, buckets either side of the brown stone sink, a small Belling cooker on a stand. The floor was slabbed, and the absence of any mat, table-cloth or cushion gave the room the feeling of being another lean-to.

Calling still, he went from room to room, walking into each so he was sure no one was hiding, or lying on the floor, in any of them. It was a voyage of some discoveries; he soon felt he pried into a very tender heart. The old man's bedroom was neat and tidy, but the bed bore a terribly faded pink bedspread and eider-down. The threadbare carpet had also been a floral pink. The chairs in the sitting room too were covered in floral cretonne; one of these to the right of the fireplace was really soiled, the other looked as if it was only the dust of time and the fading of sunlight that had affected it.

The place gave him the feeling that it had been gone through with a brush and dustpan, as one might sweep up a yard. The caring love, and polishing bit, the woman's touch, had been missing for a long time. The exceptions to this were two brass frames on the mantelpiece – these shone bright enough to gladden the heart of any army sergeant. He was guilty of forgetting his mission as he went to look at the photographs: a young, upstanding Alan Hoskins in army uniform, with a young woman who hung smiling and shy on his arm. A slightly later portrait of the same couple on holiday at the seaside, then it seemed nothing more – just a long lonely life. He closed the door very gently after himself, repenting the times he had wished the old man back to this solitary cottage, instead of last customer in his bar.

So did he tell the police? How much could he tell them? Would Alan Hoskins thank him if there were just a simple explanation? He rang Liz.

'Have a good look round outside just to make sure he's not fallen anywhere near the house, then come back.'

By lunchtime John had been back to the cottage twice, and was about to suggest his next trip should be to the nearest manned police station, when two strangers walked into the bar. They were by no means usual customers. At this time of year it was just workmen who happened to be in the area, or elderly local couples having a change from home cooking.

These two wore black overcoats over pinstriped suits, and were the kind who in John's experience frequented city gyms or expensive clubs where illegal bare-fisted boxing bouts took place.

'Good morning, gentlemen,' he said as they came to the counter.

'Good morning, landlord,' the taller of the two said, eyes having assessed the other customers, adding, 'Something to eat and drink then.'

They seated themselves at the far corner of the dining area. Liz took drinks and the menu over to their table. John watched as they kept her talking, one of them pulling papers from his inside pocket. He saw Liz's manner change from politeness, to interest – and to caution. She looked at a series of leaflets from the taller man, then shook her head, said something and with a look indicated

John. She came back to the bar, her eyes holding his, conveying more meaning than her words. 'The two gentlemen are looking for various properties in the area. They may not necessarily be for sale now, but they may have been in the last few years. Can we help them with directions?'

He understood Liz's look. What was such a request really about?

He went over to the table. 'Can I help you, gentlemen?'

The main spokesman, whose pallor and heavy jowls were slightly more endearing than the same on the acne-scarred face of the lesser man, said he hoped so. They were looking for a property in the area for a client.

He handed over the thin sheaf of papers. 'Can you give us directions to these properties?'

John looked at a series of what appeared to be property agents' advertising pamphlets. He leafed through them quickly to check that the top one, which had a pencilled date on one corner for three years before, was not just an odd one out. 'These are all big places – some I'm sure are sold.' He made to hand the papers back but the spokesman of the two held up a restraining hand. 'No,' he said, 'we still need to look over these places.'

There were two properties, Creighton Hall and Levington Manor, which were both within half an hour's drive of The Trap, but neither had villages with names associated with them, so weren't easy to find if you didn't know the area.

John made a pretence of studying the handouts, while he tried to make a reasoned reassessment of the men: dealers looking for a big property for a footballing legend or a pop star; private detectives following a lead for a client with serious money; minders? He came back to his first gut reaction: that they were sidekicks of big-time operators in some criminal racket.

He selected the details of a large property some fifty-odd miles away. 'Now I do know this,' he enthused. 'I went to a contents sale there, picked up a few pieces, a pew seat and some nice crockery for the pub.' Without any visible movement from either man he sensed their impatience with his gossip. 'But that I know must have been six or seven years ago.'

He saw a swift look pass between the two and knew his pretended prattling had in fact told them something of interest.

He obliged by drawing a basic map on the back of the details. Before he handed it and the rest of the leaflets back he riffled through them again to confirm what he found surprising – that not a single one of them had a map, or road numbers, or instructions to enable anyone to find and view.

Liz came now with soup and a basket of bread.

'Thank you, my darling,' the spokesman murmured, catching and squeezing her elbow, and with a look that had nothing to do with soup added, 'We might come back for seconds.'

John leaned over the table and put his hand flat and firm on the papers. 'You're in quite the wrong area,' he said, and before he raised his hand from their table added, 'mates.'

'Yours is she?' The lesser of the men spoke for the first time, and they both laughed.

John left them to the meal, knowing he had made the cardinal mistake of letting the opposition know what and who you really cared about.

Two more couples, all friends, who often dropped in mid-week for a meal, kept Liz busy in the kitchen. They did not have time to exchange views until John went through to report that the property seekers had gone.

'I got their car number,' Liz reported.

'So did I. Once a copper …' he began, though thinking of his own heavy hand descending on the papers, not such a smart one.

It was not until after they had locked the pub door for the afternoon that Liz said, 'Those leaflets, they wouldn't be issued by any estate agent like that.'

'No,' he agreed, 'they've been scanned into a computer and the exact locations taken out, then they've been reprinted. But why?'

'Whoever did the reprints needed to keep some kind of record, but didn't want anyone else to know,' she guessed.

'Could be, and now someone has sent their henchmen to find out,' he said.

'There's another thing,' she said with that hint of excitement, a renewal of that thirst for adventure that had made her a natural choice for special duties. He followed her to the kitchen carrying the last of the dirty cutlery and plates, and was glad no one could ask her to volunteer these days.

'I know I kept it.' She went to rummage in the dresser drawer, and after riffling about in a plethora of order pads and recipe books, she came up with a beer mat. 'Yes, look.'

He tried to share the moment of discovery, but her enthusiasm was making him wary. He glanced at a few biro strokes under the central advert for Lincolnshire Life Ales.

'Yes?' he queried.

'This is what I could make out of what was biroed on the back of the girl's hand the night we found her. I copied it at the time. It was mostly washed away, but look.' She snatched up the telephone pad and wrote down the names of the two nearest properties, Creighton Hall and Levington Manor. 'You see the loops up and down, and the dot. It could be …' She repeated the pattern of lines from the mat below both the names. 'Well,' she sounded disappointed, 'I suppose the loop at the beginning could be either a "C" or an "L", and the dot above the "i" would be in much the same place.'

'And the two strokes at the beginning of the second word could be either an "H" or an "M", Hall or Manor, so …'

'It could be either of them. Blow,' she said mildly.

'Or it could be her shopping list,' he suggested, po-faced.

'How?' she challenged, then tutted as she saw his expression.

'But at the same time,' he admitted, 'I can't think of any of the other names that came anywhere near fitting.'

'We could go and take a look-see at both these properties this afternoon,' she said, and when he looked fierce and likely to protest, she kissed him on the cheek and added, 'And look in at Alan's cottage again on the way.'

CHAPTER 5

'A FEW BRIGHT frosty days wouldn't go amiss,' John grumbled as he ran over to the car, mac loose on his shoulders.

'Never heard of February fill dyke?' Liz asked as she put the car in gear.

He leaned back in his seat, observing her pleasure in handling their classic sports car. He raised his eyebrows as she kept a straight line through deep flooded patches on the side of the empty road. 'Little things …' he began.

She laughed and swerved to take in a flood on the opposite side.

He heard again the smaller man's 'Yours is she?' He narrowed his eyes, clenched his teeth and silently confirmed the man was right. She was his.

He wondered if the story of the unnamed girl absconding from hospital in stolen clothes had hit any of the national newspapers. And had this brought the men to the area?

When they reached Hoskins' cottage, they knocked at the front door first, as John had done earlier, then went round to the back. This time the back door was locked – but the bike with the soaked saddle still leaned on the side wall, getting wetter.

'So he's been home, locked his door, and …'

'Left his bike out in this rain. How likely is that!' he exclaimed, shaking his head. 'And how far does he ever go without his bike?'

'It's hardly likely he put the bike there in the first place,' she said.

'No. It just doesn't feel right.'

'I wondered about pushing his bike under cover,' she said.

They compromised by not touching the bike but putting an upturned bucket over the saddle. It didn't feel quite so much like interfering. They could justify that neighbourly action if he came bustling in at opening time, wanting to know who'd been nosing around.

John watched the rain dripping from the bike frame. 'You don't think he's just fallen into a bog or a river and drowned?' he said, then answered his own question. 'Hardly seems likely – he knows the whole area like his own back garden.'

'There could be other family matters ...'

They were silent for a moment, considering the old man who was so vocal on some things and so quiet on others.

'I suggest we call again on our way back, and if he's still not here and doesn't turn up at opening time ...'

'And the regulars know nothing, we contact the police and make them listen,' she finished for him as they walked back to the car.

They drove on towards Creighton Hall, passing a high crumbling brick wall, reminding John of the enormous length of wall around Royal Sandringham. This boundary was not so extensive or so well maintained, but it was certainly higher. They found the front entrance to Creighton Hall marked by pillars surmounted by weather-ravaged lions holding shields with long-obliterated symbols. The huge wrought-iron gates stood open.

'So let's go calling,' she said as she turned into the drive.

It was not until the drive described a circle around a strategically placed clump of trees and rhododendrons that the house came into view.

'Bit above our social scale,' Liz added.

'Certainly a bit above our price range!'

They slowed to a crawl to admire the honey-coloured façade of the great house. A broad flight of steps led up to a pillared portico, and the steeply sloping roof was graced with three dormer windows either side of the central front door. It was grand, probably dated from around 1700, had some Dutch influences – and was not in good repair, lacking paint, and grass growing in high gutterings, blocking the flow of water and filtering it out over the edge.

'Empty,' she judged.

John walked up the steps, pulling on his gloves before he touched the large wrought-iron bell handle, another lion but rough, almost jagged, with neglect and age. There was the faint sound of the bell echoing in some distant servants' quarters, but nothing more. He tried to twist the huge knob and gave the door a hefty push with his shoulder. It did not move. 'So we'll look round the outside.'

At the back Liz followed John up a flight of stone steps to a raised terrace. 'Knew a thing or two about views,' she said, surveying the open landscape. 'Not another human dwelling in sight.'

'Somebody found it.' He beckoned her over to the French doors. There was a broken pane near the handle. He gave them a tentative push and they opened.

They stood for a moment and admired the room, the mellow gold of the floor still visible where the sun had not bleached away the colour. At intervals along each long wall were white and gilt side tables fixed to the wall, and above each one an elegant gilt-framed wall mirror.

'This must have been the ballroom.' she said. 'Look at the length and width of these old floorboards.'

'I can't believe they haven't got this place alarmed,' he said. 'It's a building reclaimer's paradise; they could make a fortune. Look at the fireplaces and the panelling, as well as all this other stuff.'

The room led through into a hall, where a magnificent oak staircase branched left and right up to a gallery.

'It doesn't look as if anything's been touched.'

'Not so far,' he said as they opened and closed doors downstairs, every sound of their careful progress magnified and thrown around in random echoes by the great empty house. 'Perhaps they were just reconnoitring,' he added.

'Like us then.' Liz led the way up the main staircase. The views from the bedroom windows were impressive, the fixtures intact but every room empty – until they came to a room at the far end of the main corridor.

In sharp contrast to everything they had seen before, this bedroom looked like an extension of a council rubbish dump. On the far wall the double doors of a large closet stood open, in front was a mass of boxes, cases and bags, which looked as if they had been pulled off the shelves, ransacked and thrown aside.

John selected a briefcase from the scattered containers. 'This looks brand new,' he said. 'Empty ... but—' he bent closer to the case '—certainly new. I can smell the leather and ... something else.'

Liz too was bending and peering in all the boxes. 'Like the house – empty,' she said.

'Not even a stray twenty pound note,' he suggested.

She looked from him back to the boxes and cases. 'Yes,' she breathed, enlightened and appalled.

'We've seen it before,' he went on, 'and if this case doesn't smell of ...'

She came across and bent over the attaché case. 'Money,' she said. 'Old, dirty money.'

They were both remembering the hundreds of thousands of pounds they had found stored in a drug dealer's bedsit. That money had been in baked bean tins and soup cartons, and all sealed round and round with parcel tape. The containers thrown about this room were more upmarket, wine and spirit boxes, and the suitcases were of decent quality and it looked as if none of them had been either sealed or locked. Whoever had put them there had been pretty confident they would not be found.

'So how much do you think this lot held?'

'Hundreds of thousands,' she guessed. 'A million? A criminal hoard either collected, or looted, in a desperate hurry – and we're now interfering with serious crime squad business.'

'Yes,' he agreed, but wanted to remind her that she had been the one wanting to delay calling the police when the girl had turned up again that morning. 'And meantime,' he added, 'we're not more than five miles from the other place, Levington Manor?'

'Why not?' she enthused. 'Might as well look at both now – as well hung for a sheep as a lamb.'

The difference between the two properties could not have been more extreme. Well before they arrived there were signs for 'Levington Manor African Violet Centre'. The signs proliferated the nearer they got, and it was obvious it was much more – garden centre, snack bar, restaurant.

'Never know what we might learn,' he said, but when the nearest car-parking spaces were full and they had to drive along a track to a second area being cleared for another car park, he grumbled and suggested they leave it.

'There's been a car behind me all the way,' she told him. 'I'll have to pull in, so we might as well stop.'

They walked back to the centre in silence, but as they entered Liz exclaimed in delight as they were confronted by seemingly endless rows of African violets in all shades from white, through the pinks and purples to the blues, light and dark.

'Can they bloom at any time of the year?' she asked of no one in particular.

'Yes, that can be managed,' a tall man with receding sandy hair told her with a grin. 'Mother's Day, 6th March, the perfect traditional present – violets.'

'Well, not *African* violets,' she said, 'but I can see their appeal.'

'Treat them right and they'll be one of the best investments in pot plants you can make.'

'How long have you been here?' John asked. 'Specializing like this?'

'Not long actually. It was a garden centre, then it stood empty for a bit. It's taken us three years to pull it back, but its been specializing that's brought the customers.' He could not keep the pride out of his voice. 'That and advertising on the net. We're applying to become an official site of special interest.'

'They're lovely,' Liz said, as they moved on, 'particularly the pink ones. Some of those would look lovely among my white pottery ducks, warm and bright, don't you think?'

'So he's been here three years, but it was empty for a time before that. Creighton Hall is empty ...'

'You're looking for a pattern, Inspector?' she queried.

'Damn it,' he admitted, 'let's go and have a cup of tea before we go back to Hoskins' place.'

In the snack bar he ordered tea and toasted teacakes. Two huge windows overlooked the arrays of violets. 'You can window shop while you're eating,' he said. 'This chap's got his head screwed on. Specialization, that's the key. We should go for renovating our stables and advertising bird-watching holidays, or painting holidays with Paul as resident tutor.'

'We said when we could afford it.' She looked at him speculatively.

'We'll definitely keep it in mind,' he said. Tea and teacakes finished, John told Liz, 'You go and fetch the car – I'll get you some pink violets.'

'Oh! Thanks,' she said, turning to give him a beaming smile before disappearing behind a little group of people at a cash-out.

He felt a stupid pang of loss when he could no longer see her, and hurried to pick up a basket. He quickly chose a dozen plants and took his selection to the counter. He paid and walked out of the garden centre, the plants balanced in a stout cardboard tray. He thought of the cardboard boxes in Creighton Hall, plundered, scattered; of Hoskins who might, or might not, be on a private errand, and of the girl running from the pub to go off with the man in the Porsche. It was all beginning to feel a little too close to home.

He looked impatiently for Liz. Knowing her she would have hurried back to the car, aware they had a lot to do before opening time. He stood and ran a scenario of flowers in the boot, mutual admiration of his choice, peck on the cheek and off they would go – to the cottage and home. If there were no news of Hoskins they would have to contact the police again. He reviewed several possible versions of how they might explain their visit to Creighton Hall, none comfortable. It was all going to be bloody awkward.

Then *he* began to feel very awkward balancing the tray of flowers, like a waiter, a disorientated waiter with refreshments for customers he's lost. 'Come on, Liz,' he urged, stepping out into the roadway so he could see further along the lane. He wasn't sure whether it was a dead end, but it was certainly deserted.

He looked back into the garden centre and realized how dark it was growing. The lights looked bright now. Inside people were drifting around the long benches of flowers, but many were disappearing through to the snackbar. It must be nearly four o'clock, British teatime, and it looked as if this was a regular outing for some people, a meeting place for tea and cakes.

He began to walk towards the second car park. A couple coming towards him made extravagant room for him and the grey-haired woman said, 'Oh! Aren't they lovely? Someone's going to be lucky.'

He nodded. 'The lady of my life,' he said without breaking his stride. 'She's supposed to be fetching the car. Red MG,' he said, looking at the man, who immediately shook his head.

It triggered a curl of cold unease at the base of his spine. He hurried on, wanting to hurl the flowers in the hedge but resisting the impulse. After all, there could be a problem with the car. The old couple could just not have seen it; a big vehicle could completely screen others from view.

Yes, he told himself, that would be it – or had it been stolen?

He stumbled on the rutted lane. What was he thinking about? If there had been a problem she would have used her mobile phone. He would have been her first call if she needed help – or she could have just walked back to him.

He dumped the tray of flowers on top of a rubbish bin just inside the second car park and ran – quicker than fumbling around with a phone.

True to his former expectation, there was a minibus screening his view of where they had parked. He hurried forward, to find a Ford Focus disgorging a family of three shaven-headed boys, miniature editions of their shaven-headed and ear-ringed father, who urged them out of the car with a hand like a shovel. Their mother stood a pace or two away, lighting a cigarette.

'What's up, mate?' the man asked as John came to a halt, staring, looking round.

'My car, it was parked here.' He pointed to the spot they were in.

'Nothin' 'ere when we arrived. Never saw nothin', did we, Angie?'

The woman inhaled and shook her head.

'Thanks, anyway,' he said, unfolding his phone and punching number one in his directory, Liz's mobile.

The family's voices retreated into the distance, and the phone still rang. Was she driving? Had he just missed her? Should he collect the plants and go back to the garden centre? 'Hell,' he breathed, 'come on, Liz, you've had time to park and answer, wherever you are.'

He began to walk as he listened, and had got to the bin and his plants when there was a click and a man's voice enquired, 'Is that the ex-fuzz?'

'Who's that?' John reacted.

'Just listen!' He recognized the voice of the bigger of the two men from lunchtime. 'You're to tell your customers and anyone who asks that the little lady has gone on holiday for a bit.'

'And why would I do that?' He kept every emotion from his voice.

'I guess because you want 'er back in one piece. So you won't be contacting any of your police friends anywhere.'

'Let me speak to her,' he demanded.

'She's tied up at the moment,' the smart-aleck other voice butted in.

'I'll hunt you to the ends of the earth if anything happens to her,' he promised.

There was a grunt of laughter. 'What makes you think you'll be luckier this time?' The voice was that of a man who knew he held the aces. 'You go back to that nice little pub, and don't go looking round any more empty properties. Keep your head down, your mouth tight shut and your pub open. We'll be watching. We'll let you know when and where you can pick your lady up. Depends on you what state she's in – we're not fussy.'

The phone went dead in his hand.

When John was dropped back at The Trap it was past opening time, and by the taxi's headlights he saw there were already two cars in his car park. He had just spent the longest, loneliest two hours of his life forcing himself to think more like a trained police officer than he had ever done before.

As the taxi swept around, lighting the front of the pub, a man stepped out of the porch.

'John? Is everything all right?' Paul Jefferson called. 'I've been to Hoskins' place and that's deserted, then I come here and this place is in darkness. Your car's here, then you arrive in a taxi?'

'My car?' he snapped.

'Your MG,' he began, 'I parked next to it. I ...' But John was running and Jefferson followed to where the two cars were parked side by side. 'What's going on?' he asked as John tried to open the door of the MG.

'I need a light,' he said.

Without another word Paul went to his own car boot, unlocked it and brought out a lamp. John snatched it from him. He shone the light into the interior of the MG.

On the back seat was Liz's red purse, its contents, coins, credit cards scattered around, along with a spare red bobble. She usually had one of those in her purse.

'Not like Liz to ...' Paul began, then drew in his breath as John lurched past him from door to boot, and with an effort of will raised the lid and looked inside. It was empty but his knees needed the support of the car bumper to keep him upright.

'Christ!' Paul's blasphemy was awed. 'What did you expect to find?'

John closed the boot, staggered and as Paul gripped his arm to steady him, snatched away. 'Let's get inside,' he said.

'I must hurry,' he said, the lamp heavy, its light erratic as he led the way at a wobbly-kneed sprint. He unlocked the back door, switching on every light as he went through to the bar, then the outside floodlights before he went to unlock the front door.

Jefferson had followed, completely bemused, but when John finally stopped, breathless and deathly pale by the bar, Jefferson closed his sagging mouth, went to the optics, put a brandy in a glass and gave it to him.

'Liz has been called away,' he said as a car stopped outside and doors slammed.

'Right,' Jefferson said, disbelieving, but getting the message. 'A bereavement, by the look of you. If you want to go and collect yourself I'll look after the bar – worked my way through art college behind a bar.'

'God, could you? give me ...'

'A chance to think.'

He nodded. 'Thanks,' he said, adding, 'Yes, make it a family illness.'

'Right.'

'I'll come in ...'

Jefferson raised a hand that said whenever he felt up to it. 'I've no one waiting for me.'

He got out of the bar, taking the brandy with him just before he recognized the accents of local men greeting Jefferson.

'What, old Hoskins not here yet!' one exclaimed.

'Where's John?' asked the other.

He's trying to raise his bloody friend in the Met, he silently answered, as again he punched the keys of his mobile.

CHAPTER 6

I
T WAS JEFFERSON who saw the last customers from the bar at closing time, with a quip about the boss making him stay to wash up, then he turned to face John. 'So?' he queried.

After a night of questions, answered with lies evoking quiet words of sympathy and messages to convey to Liz, this one blunt word was like the end of the line, the buffers, the time for the truth.

But before John could make any kind of reply, he realized that Jefferson was moving towards the switches to turn off the bar lights.

'No!' he shouted, then as the startled man turned, he repeated in a lower voice, 'No, I need them to all stay on, while I ask a lot more of you than washing up.'

Leaving the lights, the bar and the front door all as if customers still lingered, John led the way to the kitchen. 'I've made strong coffee.'

Fifteen minutes later he finished the story with an account of his phone call to Angus Austin in Dorset about his son Robert.

'Hello, dear boy,' the barrister had greeted. 'Long time no see. Robert? Weekend sabbatical he said, when his mama wanted him to come down. He'll be holed up in that flat of his, ignoring all calls.'

This had been all John had wanted to know, and all Paul needed to be told, as he dropped his car keys into John's hand.

John put on Jefferson's anorak and headed for the car, giving a fair imitation of a man who had perhaps had just a little too much to drink to be driving. He wasn't sure if The Trap was being watched but he was taking no chances. By the time he had reversed and was leaving the car park, the outside lights of the pub went out, as did the front bar lights. Paul had timed that just right, just like the action of a landlord glad to be rid of a lingering customer. He thanked all the deities mankind believed in for this trusting, intelligent artist, so willing to help in circumstances most men would run a mile from. 'I hope to drive back into the car park tomorrow evening at opening time,' he had told him.

There had been only one question Jefferson had asked that he could not answer. 'So where's Hoskins?'

Once out of the confines of his home area, he set about putting Jefferson's Peuguot through its paces. He was thankful now for a dark, cold, wet February night that kept people at home. He drove with concentrated speed along the lanes to join the A1067 to Norwich. He ignored the ring road and drove straight through the centre. He watched the floodlit cathedral drop behind him. Was he doing the right thing?

He knew he'd been recognized. Ex-fuzz, he'd been called, then there was that significant 'What makes you think you'll be luckier this time?' These men were from his past, from his time in the Met. Then there was the girl – they had both heard the tones of a true Cockney in her 'Nah!' as she was asked if anyone would miss her. 'Nah! It was all well planned.'

John had to plan even more carefully, and fear for Liz suddenly took his breath. 'Oh God,' he gasped. There was so much that could go wrong. He needed an awful lot of luck on his side to even begin to make this mad dash to the far side of London worthwhile.

Between Colchester and Chelmsford he made good time on near-deserted roads, reached the outskirts of the city at three in the morning, and Austin's apartment in Islington just after four. He stood in the doorway and kept his finger on the bell push until a terse 'Yes' told him Robert Auguste Austin was at home.

'John Cannon,' he announced just as tersely.

There was the slightest of pauses then the front door clicked and allowed him access. When he reached the first-floor apartment, Austin was at the door in his dressing gown. A man whose compact broadness belied his six foot, Cannon had always felt that Austin should have been superintendent to his inspector rather than his run-around sergeant – now the relationship seemed more natural. A quiet man with a natural authority, he thrust out a hand and drew John into his home. Then his greeting became a brief embrace.

'Good to see you, but the hour states trouble. So?'

John suddenly felt unutterably weary as the same short word Jefferson had used in the pub bar half a lifetime ago now prompted him on the same retelling – well, not quite the same. This man had powers beyond goodwill and friendship.

They went through to the lounge. Austin took his anorak, holding it aloft and frowning at it. 'Where's the mac? Liz surely hasn't let you part with it.'

Austin went to sit at a large antique partner's desk (his father's until he retired from Chambers) and began to make notes. Cannon paced the room and talked.

'So you have the number of the Rover the two men drove,' Austin said. 'Give it to me.'

Austin put through an immediate call, and within a couple of minutes he dropped the receiver. 'Hire car from a garage near one of those big private car parks serving Heathrow.'

'So ...' John began.

'You know hot cars are dumped on those long-stay car parks for months. They could have just done a swap for this hire job, but—' he paused to nod at his old boss '—it does mean you were right to come.'

John read the held glance and knew he was giving him reassurance of his wholesale help. 'Thanks, Austin,' he said earnestly.

Austin cleared his throat, suddenly much more like his English father than his French mother, as he went on, 'It appears whatever is going on in your backwater could be London based.'

'Mugshots?' John suggested.

'Yes,' he agreed, 'that's the next step.' Together they went through John's description of the men in detail, and in the order they would appear on the records – ethnicity, age, height, build, hair, clothing – then Austin went to the telephone again. 'I'll set this up, save time when we get there. Don't you want a drink?'

He ached to follow the gesture to the sideboard and have a large single malt in one of Austin's crystal glasses, but knew he could not afford the indulgence of a temporary lift; he had to stay alert for a long time yet. 'Stomach's awash with coffee. Think I should eat something,' he said. Austin pointed towards the kitchen as he asked to be put through to 'Jim'.

John pondered not for the first time that the Met was a strange old place. Everyone knew a few people really well, and others could be complete strangers because duties and shifts never coincided.

He ate a crust of bread plastered with brie from the fridge as he foraged, then carried two apples back into the sitting room to listen to the progress Austin was making.

He was putting the phone down as he entered. 'We can leave at once,' he said, 'and we'll go in your car. You may not want to come back here afterwards. But I'll drive, you can nibble.'

As they joined the sparse traffic of early morning, John found himself shaking his head at the experience of being driven through his old everyday haunts. His eyes snatched at the familiar, but used now to lanes, tracks, small town centres, the scale of streets and buildings were alien, out of proportion, the old scenario too large.

'All right?' Austin queried.

'Feel a bit like Alice down the rabbit hole.'

'Yes,' Austin hissed quiet understanding, then asked, 'The girl who came back to the pub – tell me everything you can remember about her, everything she said.'

Austin mused that tattooed bracelets were quite usual, but a plain wedding-ring tattoo was not, and with the newspaper picture, they should identify her without delay if she was on their records.

'So you think all the events are connected?'

'Not answering that yet,' Austin said. 'The suited man who encountered your old poacher …'

'Hoskins,' John supplied.

'Does not appear to have anything at all to do with your two heavies, but he certainly has with the girl and the man in the Porsche. To be honest …'

John heard the beginning of the 'sir'.

'Old habits … sir,' Austin said, then continued, 'To be honest, I think we should involve your local force in finding the Porsche and the Rover.'

John felt the adrenaline pump and lost what Austin was saying for a few seconds.

'Just a sighting order, motor patrols trawl a wide sea, then if either are seen, time and place to be called in immediately – but no further action.'

John thought of the youngster who had surmised he could not hack the Met, and ruminated on the consequences of some over-diligent young cop getting it wrong. He brushed a hand over his forehead, over icy-cold sweat.

'We need to draw information on all aspects from all sources,' Austin said in a reasoned way, and with aggravation he knew that Austin, the academic, would now give his reasons. He did, all of which John could have recited with him. He stared fixedly through the windscreen.

'John!' Austin now pronounced his name like a wake-up call. 'These men are on some kind of mission – in, hit, out – you know how they work. They'll not hold Liz for long, she's a hindrance, and they're gambling on you caring enough about her to keep quiet.'

'That's hardly a gamble,' he said. 'I played into their hands.'

Austin's silence was a question in itself.

'I showed how I felt about Liz.'

'No change there then,' Austin said.

The remark, and the fact that his old sergeant swung round into John's old parking space, gave him pause for further thought. 'Was I that transparent?' he asked but not loud enough to be heard.

'I've got a screen show set up in one of the interview rooms, and …' Austin paused at a door to verify his identity. 'I do have good contacts on the Lincolnshire and Norfolk forces.'

He nodded, knowing full well that sighting would also mean keeping tabs on. It all made good police sense but he still hated the idea.

Austin ushered him to the computer room. 'You begin, I'll leave you for a few minutes. Start another search on the girl with this—' he wagged the newspaper John had brought from home '—and the information you've given me.'

John knew for certain he was also going to set up the across-county observation orders for the two cars. Distracted, he had rolled down several pictures without seeing them and had to return to the beginning. He had prayed for a quick outcome, but as he scrolled on and on through the mugshots, his hopes receded. The best matches were usually first, and by the time he had sat in concentrated silence for twenty minutes he knew he was not going to get a result.

Austin had been back by his side some time when the rogues' gallery came to an end.

'I've found nothing on the girl either, but there's a lot more we can do on her. I've got a man working on it now. If what she told you is true, there's her brother killed in a road accident after a drug investigation at his school. Individually almost everyday events, but if they were linked this could give us a lead. Did she give any indication what area she came from? Was London even mentioned?'

'Again it's nothing more than impressions, her designer clothes, most of all though her accent, true Cockney, I would have said, with a few of the rough edges rubbed off, but still a touch of Bow Bells ... but I'm clutching at straws.'

'Yes,' Austin agreed. 'Any and all of them. Stacks are built of straws.'

'But where do I go from here?' John asked.

'You have to be back at the pub by ...' Austin broke off and frowned at him. 'I always thought you did lunches?'

'I arranged for a notice on the pub door to say no lunchtime openings for the time being due to family illness. But I aim to be the first customer at six tonight, exchange places with Jefferson.'

Austin nodded. 'So you need to time your return just right.'

He was wondering if Austin was going to suggest taking him back to his apartment when there was a knock on the door. A shirt-sleeved man, who looked as if he was probably near the end of his thirty years' police service, as well as near the end of his shift, came in.

He nodded at John then shook straight a thin dossier of sagging papers before handing them to Austin. 'The girl herself, nothing has come up, but I've found two boys accidentally killed running away from their schools, allegedly because of a police presence, one ten years ago, one seven years ago.'

'Thanks, Jeff, thanks for your help.'

When he'd gone Austin scrutinized the reports, handing each sheet to John as he finished with it.

The first dealt with a twelve-year-old who had run from school when sniffer dogs had been taken in. 'No mention of parents,' Austin commented, 'or a sister come to that, but a possible.'

The second fatality was that of a boy off the Old Kent Road, who had been changing classrooms mid-morning when he and other pupils had seen two police cars arrive. The boy, Brian Starmer, had just walked off, but had not arrived at their next lesson; then had been seen running from the school premises. He had been hit by a bus. His sister, Tracey Starmer, had said that whatever drug problem they might have at the school she knew for certain her brother was not involved.'

'Eureka?' Austin suggested.

'Good chance,' John agreed, wondering if at last their girl had a name. Tracey Starmer.

'We've time to go to the Old Kent Road,' Austin suggested.

'Right,' John agreed, the idea that he should grab a couple of hours lying down before driving back to Lincolnshire banished.

'I'll get us a car,' Austin said. 'Won't risk your friend's.'

They found that Tracey Starmer lived in a first-floor council-owned flat. They went through the formalities of knocking and ringing her doorbell, and the other flat door on the same landing, with the same negative result.

But as they came down the concrete stairs and out a side door, a grey-haired little woman, scrawny as a London sparrow, stood outside the block talking to a man, about her age, not much taller, but looking as if he had retired from a long career in the boxing ring.

'Who y're wanting?' he asked.

'You live here?' Austin asked.

'Nah!' he laughed and looked at John. 'But I know the Old Bill when I sees 'em. Y're lookin' for somebody.'

'We're looking for Tracey Starmer,' Austin said.

'She's away,' the woman put in. 'Left me her key and a month's rent money – said she wasn't sure how long she'd be away.'

The man gave a snort of disapproval.

'Do you know Tracey?' Austin asked.

'Everyone knows Tracey around 'ere,' he replied. 'Her parents before 'er – and her brother,' he added with meaning.

'The boy who was killed in a road accident.'

'S'right,' he said. 'You'd know all about that.'

Austin ignored the challenge in his voice and produced a copy of the newspaper picture. 'Is this Tracey?'

'Christ!' the old lady exclaimed and appealed to her friend. 'It is 'er, ain't it, Charlie, but she d'on 'alf look bad.'

'What's 'appened to 'er?' Charlie asked.

'That's what we're trying to find out. If you could tell us more about her, where she works, for instance, who her friends are, it could help us a lot.'

The four of them were soon in the old lady's flat with cups of tea and a formidable array of biscuits and cakes conjured from various tins and packets. Only when she had exhausted the range she could find to offer did she sit down.

'Tracey used to work for me,' Charlie told them. 'I 'ad a pub further along the road 'ere till I retired. 'Ad a good clientele from the boxing world.'

'How long ago was that?'

'Oh! 'Til one of them fancy bistro-cum-wine bars opened the other side the Elephant & Castle. Well, she got more hours there than I could give 'er, so I didn't see so much of 'er, but she's a good kid. Kept 'er brother out of a 'ome when they were left on their own. Then four years later 'e gets killed by a bleeding bus.'

'Would you know the name of this bistro?'

The woman got up and rummaged in a sideboard drawer, bringing out several books of matches. 'She brought me a few of these,' she said and gave Austin and John a packet each.

'The Airy Dungeon,' John read, and looked at the address. 'This must be near the Imperial War Museum.'

'S'right,' Charlie acknowledged.

'She's not in any trouble, is she?' the woman asked, passing gingernuts and chocolate digestives.

'As far as we know she has done nothing wrong,' Austin said, 'but we are concerned for her safety.'

'Bleedin' knew it!' Charlie exclaimed and turned to the woman. 'What did I say? When some geezer drops 'er off round the corner so no one can see who 'e is? 'Im in 'is bleeding Porsche!'

CHAPTER 7

JOHN WOKE WITH a start. For seconds he did not know where he was, why he had a polystyrene beaker of coffee balancing between his thighs, or what the insistent noise was.

'Get a new mobile, let me have the number and keep it exclusively for me.' Austin's words. 'I'll keep you informed. Everything I find out you'll know.'

He had called at a phone warehouse and phoned Austin with the new number before he left the city environs, before he hit the motorway home, before he stopped at a service station for coffee.

He snapped his wrist round to look at his watch: 1500 hours. He had three hours to get back to The Trap and where was he? He couldn't think for the ridiculous noise the phone was making in his pocket – a free trial ringtone for a month. It jangled round his head like toothache as he struggled to put the coffee on the floor and extricate the fold-up phone from the anorak pocket.

'Are you all right?' Austin asked, as he prised his tongue from the roof of his mouth to answer.

'Sure, just stopped for a coffee.'

'I've seen the wine-bar manager where Tracey worked mornings and evenings, and found out she also worked afternoons in a tattoo parlour in the next street. The manager said occasionally a toff came in, had just one small glass of wine, and talked to Tracey. The tattooist was the most interesting. He had seen neither a man nor a Porsche, but he said Tracey had come in all excited one afternoon, bringing a design, properly detailed, for a tattoo of a wedding ring. "It was a symbol," Tracey said.'

'The same words she used to me,' John remembered.

'So the same man she ran to outside your pub?' Austin suggested.

'Right,' he agreed, 'if we could trace his Porsche ...'

'Taking a circle from Tracey's home and places of work, we are already tracing, interviewing and eliminating from enquiries all Porsche owners. I'll keep you posted.'

'Thanks,' he said, feeling the one word was inadequate as Austin rang off. He bent to retrieve and drink the cold coffee and register that the service station he was on was the London side of Ipswich.

He swung over into the fast lane as soon as he saw a gap in the traffic. He drove with determined concentration but with a sense of failure. What he had hoped to achieve was some breakthrough about the two men who held Liz. Instead he had a new mobile in his pocket and a direct line to the police he had been warned not to contact. Someone hooted at him irritably as he continued to straddle a lane marker.

The front door of the public house was open, the floodlights and the bar lights on when he swung back in next to their red MG, otherwise he was relieved to see the car park was empty.

He walked into the bar and he and Paul Jefferson confronted each other like men returned from perilous journeys to opposite poles.

'Good timing,' Paul said.

'I owe you – big time.' He felt the remark was trite, tried to expand but Paul waved it away.

'You look out on your feet,' he said.

John's nod included the unspoken comment that Paul didn't look much better.

'I didn't sleep much,' he acknowledged, 'and we had visitors.

Quite a few people came at lunchtime, but they just read the notice and went away. Then two men in a black Rover, they parked next to your MG, and had a good look round it before walking towards the pub. They were the men you described.'

John registered the other man's heavy swallow and the glance towards the counter before Paul said, 'I went and stood behind the front door thinking they would be sure to make some remark when they read the notice.'

Again the glance to the counter, which as far as he could see had only the usual beer mats and the vase of fresh flowers Liz always kept at one end. 'They must have separated and one walked round the back,' Paul was saying, 'because it was quite a few minutes before they re-met at the front door. I heard one say that there was a light on upstairs so he thought you were here. The other said you'd better be, but to leave you the reminder to keep your mouth tight shut.'

Paul paused to pinch and knead his bottom lip. 'When that letterbox yawned opened, I felt as if I was in the middle of a stage. It seemed to take hours not seconds for them to—' He turned and picked up something from behind the flowers on the bar '—push this through.'

Jefferson held out a brown A4 envelope.

There was no name on it, nothing, but it had been used before, was crumpled, stained, bulky and the roughly torn top was just folded over.

John's hand shook as he reached for it.

'It wasn't sealed so I have looked. It's … disturbing.'

He took the envelope, unfolded the top, and put pressure on the sides so he could see inside without touching. He frowned, unable to make sense of the contents. He stepped over to a table and tipped the envelope.

A mass of hair, a twist of red and a photograph slid on to the gleaming mahogany surface. The red was one of those elasticated hair bobbles. She wouldn't need it now, he thought. He heard

Jefferson say something, swear, blaspheme, and registered this was what he should be doing, but he hardly felt he was on the same planet. This must be what it was like to die, he thought, to be there, but not to be any more – all emotion for the moment spent.

Automatically he reached for the photograph and turned it face side up. A woman – Liz – bound in a sitting position at the base of a set of sturdy open steps, the kind found in barns. Her head was up, her roughly shorn hair hanging at the level of the hollows below her cheekbones. She was gagged but her eyes had caught the flash of the camera and he read only defiance.

'They'll pay,' he said, and found himself at the counter, beating his fists down again and again, each time repeating, 'They'll pay,' until Paul caught one arm. 'No, I'll kill …' He tried to pull away but Paul insisted. 'No, listen!'

There were other voices outside, customers, men calling on their way home from work, about to walk into the public bar, and it felt like the most extraordinary intrusion.

Paul nodded towards the table. John put the photograph into his pocket as Paul, with a brief look of apology, unceremoniously slid the hair and bobble back into the envelope and handed it to him. Then he gestured John in the direction of the private quarters. 'Take my anorak off,' he said, 'and get a shave.' When he hesitated, Paul added, 'Look, I'm in this with you now – all the way.'

'You still on duty?' John heard one of the early customers ask.

'Can't do too much for a good boss,' Paul said. 'Pint, is it, Buddy?'

Buddy Brompton and his companion were both lorry drivers, working from a local depot delivering crops from the rich soils around The Wash to all parts of the UK and beyond – and regular customers for a pint or two on their way home. John frowned as he heard them enquiring about Hoskins; for him this was one worry too far. He took out his new phone and pressed Austin's number.

Austin answered almost at once but cut across anything John

was going to say. 'I'm with the chief. Leave me a message – I'll get back to you ASAP. Right?'

'Right.' The dial tone snapped back in. John knew better than to be offended. He sat at the kitchen table, tapped in a text message and, propping the photograph against a milk bottle, he carefully focused and sent Austin a copy of that too. Photo of a photo would not be good, but good enough to make Austin fully understand the situation.

He showered, shaved and changed in less than half an hour and was just joining Paul behind the bar when the new phone announced a text message. 'Recd yrs. Things afoot. Open pub 2mrow lunch.'

'All right?' Paul asked.

'Open pub tomorrow lunchtime?' he queried, turning the message so Paul could read it.

'"Things afoot?"' Paul picked out. 'What sort of language is that these days?'

'It will exactly describe what's happening,' he defended, though his first thought had been to ring back and demand more information.

'You trust him?'

'I am,' he said, 'with Liz's life,' only too aware of how true that was and how it was far too late for moments of doubt.

'Christ!' The blasphemy was breathed low as two more customers walked into the bar, first greeting the two at the table before coming to the bar.

'Evening,' one said, nodding to Jefferson. The other took in John's appearance. 'Not had a funeral have you, John? You know, Liz's relation?'

'Very tactful,' his companion commented.

'No, well, we heard – and he looks a bit washed out.'

'No,' John said. 'You're all right. I'm just tired.'

'Hope you'll soon have some good news,' the enquirer said, picking up his pint and moving over to join their friends.

'And so say all of us,' Paul murmured.

Buddy and his fellow lorry driver had rather uncharacteristically retreated to a table in the far corner. The four were all regulars from round about; Buddy and one of the two newcomers were both members of the darts team.

The distance between table and counter left John and Paul free to talk.

'I've nothing to go home for,' Paul said. 'I could stay again tonight.'

'That poses the problem of your car being here all night,' John said. 'We can't risk anything that might make those men think something out of the ordinary is happening, but ...'

'I'll come over lunchtime then, shall I?' Paul was saying as Buddy came up to the counter with empty glasses.

Something in the man's approach alerted both men behind the counter. He looked like a man with news of some import to convey, and the way the other three at the table were watching him seemed to indicate that he came not just for refills but as spokesman for them all.

He had raised the empty glasses to the level of the counter, opened his mouth to order, when the bar door burst open so violently it banged back on its hinges and would have closed again had there not been several other men on the heels of the first.

'Gi' us a brandy,' the first man said, half falling across the counter.

'Gi' us all a brandy,' the next said, indicating his other two companions.

'Four brandies coming up,' Paul said, turning to the optics.

'What's up?' Buddy asked.

The men looked from one to the other. 'Hell!' one said with the conviction of one who had evidence.

'Hell!' another confirmed.

Another blew out his cheeks, looked across at John and said, 'Wouldn't be a copper for all the tea in China.'

'Not with jobs like that to do.' The man downed his brandy and pushed it across to Paul with a nod to the optics.

'Jobs like what?' Buddy asked impatiently. 'What?'

'Bodies,' he replied enigmatically. 'Bloody bodies.'

'Body,' another corrected. 'A bloody body.'

The four nodded, heads in unison, at this summing up.

'It's Hoskins,' Buddy said. 'Knew something had happened. We'd just decided we were going to the police, hadn't we?' He turned back to his table to have his story confirmed, but the men were on their way to the counter to hear the men at closer range.

'Where was he?'

'Noo!' The denial was a chorus.

'Not Hoskins?'

'Near his place, but ...'

'How near?'

'Not Hoskins?'

'The way he'd go home, and the way old Hoskins always told it.' The man paused to nod at the empty pew-like seat where the old poacher usually sat. 'It's about where he found that girl he went on about.'

'Girl?' John's voice rose above all like the voice of God.

There was an immediate silence, all eyes now focused on the landlord.

'That's right,' the man who'd crashed open the door confirmed. 'A girl, a woman.' He paused, his intended shrug turning to a shudder. 'But I'll tell you one thing for sure – there's nothing accidental about the way she died.'

John barely remembered leaving the pub, had no memory of running, only of arriving at the same gateway where Hoskins had found Tracey Starmer wet through and unconscious. Here there were now three police cars, searchlights and a tent being erected over most of the gateway, plus the inevitable three or four cars belonging to the concerned or the curious.

CHAPTER 8

'KEEP BACK, SIR.' A uniformed arm came hard and firm across his chest, and for a second he relived the times he had kept anxious relatives away from disaster scenes – times when the concerned tried to force a way through, even threw a blow at the person trying to stop them, as he nearly did now.

'I'm looking for my partner,' he said. 'She's ...'

'What, sir? She's ... what?' A more authoritative voice asked and a plain-clothes man came into the circle of light.

'You are?' he asked.

'Detective Sergeant Maddern,' the man answered, then looking closer at John asked, 'Don't I know you, sir?'

'Licensee of The Trap with my partner, Liz. She's away ...' The automatic spiel of lies made him feel unreal, playing a part. 'Expected back. Some customers came in, said there'd been a woman ...'

'Your partner would be driving home, no doubt,' the sergeant said. 'This is not a road traffic accident.'

'She might have come on a bus and walked from the bus stop,' he continued on as he remembered this was what Tracey Starmer had done when she'd come back to the pub. 'I need to know if it's my partner.'

'John?' a man in a dark overcoat queried, as he came from the taped-off area, and Cannon tried to force his way in. He caught John in his arms, repeating his name. 'John! John Cannon!' In the tussle between the two, John forced his way clear, caught the smell of blood, bruised grass, sodden soil – and in a spotlight saw the figure at the butt of the tree, saw that not only had life gone, but whoever had killed her had done so with the most malicious force. The face was reduced to bloody anonymity, as were the hands, which would no doubt have been raised to shield the face.

The man who held him continued to say his name, and he realized it was their local doctor. He and Liz had come to know him and his wife Jane as good customers and friends. Dr Purdy relaxed his hold as John stopped struggling. 'No doubt your pathologist, Sergeant, will soon be here, so I'll get on. I've a surgery full of patients waiting.'

'Look, John,' Dr Purdy tried to reassure him. 'She was dead hours before I was summoned – and look how short her hair is …'

'Her hair!' John heard a groan like a mortally wounded animal break from his lips, and would have fallen to his knees had the doctor not thrust his own body forward to support him.

'Look at her feet, man,' he urged. 'Those shoes can't be more than a four. At Liz's height she must take at least a six or seven. Yes!' He urged the truth of this on his distraught companion.

John looked back and the doctor moved a constable aside so he could see the feet, one stretched out straight, the other protruding so the sole of the shoe was visible under the calf of the first leg.

The sole of the boot was tiny compared with those he had so often stood upright in their porch. 'Yes,' he admitted, drawing a shuddering breath like a swimmer coming up after too long under water.

'Come on, I'll drive you back,' the doctor said.

'I just need a minute,' John procrastinated.

'Did you expect Liz back tonight?' Dr Purdy asked as he shepherded Cannon to his car.

'No,' he said carefully, 'not necessarily.'

'That girl had been killed where she was, that's for sure,' the doctor said as he stopped the car at The Trap.

'Not dumped from a car?' John asked.

'No.' The doctor was certain. 'Anyway, I thought you two had left police work behind you.'

John attempted a laugh. 'It sort of creeps back up on you sometimes.'

'Take care then.' The doctor gave him a salute. 'Remember me to Liz. We must come over for a meal again soon.'

John stood and watched the car go, then turned and walked into his bar. The two men at the counter and Paul stopped their conversation mid-word, and gazed fixedly at him.

'All right?' Paul asked.

He nodded, then asked, 'Where are the others?'

'They went after you,' Paul told him. 'Didn't you see them?'

He shook his head.

'You need a holiday, mate,' one of two remaining customers said, downing his pint and giving the nod to his mate. 'See you,' he said as they both left.

'You thought it might be Liz,' Paul said, 'but it obviously wasn't, so who…?'

John shook his head.

'Road accident?'

John shook his head with slower but greater emphasis. 'Murder,' he said. 'Awful bloody murder.'

'Murder …' Paul began then, trying to reason it out, added, 'Of course, it could perhaps be what you police call a domestic.'

'But …' John's turn now to do the reasoning. 'The men holding Liz are going to see police swarming all over the area and wonder if I've …'

'Spilled the beans,' Paul realized, knuckles pounding his lips. John was already reaching into his pocket for his phone.

'Austin,' the tone of voice conjured an intense listening silence as he relayed the evening's events.

Paul came round to pace the bar, listening first to the phone call, then to make sure no customers were approaching.

'Yes,' he said at length, 'No ... too many people know already. I agree. Can I ... no ... Right,' and the phone was folded.

'He says for once the media circus has to be kicked into action. Before the night's out he'll make sure there are announcements about the finding of the girl's body on radio and TV. We're to do nothing, except listen and watch. Make sure the announcement is made, get back to him if it's not.'

'So we just have to hope the bastards holding Liz listen to or watch the news? Paul said grimly.

'If they're professionals they listen to everything, police transmissions, the lot,' he said.

'You think these are?'

'They have all the hallmarks, so ...' He broke off.

'So?' Paul dropped a heavy fist on to the counter as the abstraction continued. 'So!'

'I think it's unlikely they murdered that woman.' John looked up, the memory of the woman in his eyes. 'Whoever did that was in a frenzy of passionate hate. Not how professional killers go about things, risking getting splattered with their victim's blood.'

Paul swore quietly. 'I wonder you ever wanted to be a lawman,' he said. 'I'm glad I chose the arts. So is there anything else we can do?'

'Continue the pretence that Liz is away, and act normally.'

'Christ!' Paul said vehemently. 'You mean just sweat it out until tomorrow lunchtime, and hope to God your friend has come up with something positive.'

'I can't think what else to do,' John said, his voice almost inaudible as he added, 'Not a single thing that would help.'

Paul gripped his arm. 'Guess your London friend would say "They also serve who only stand and wait".'

'I reckon.'

Customers began to trickle in again as the evening went on, and all the talk was of the girl. At half past nine someone came in with the news of a suspicious death on the local radio. 'It's just up the road, did you know?' He was loudly assured that everyone did know, but as the time ran up to ten John fetched his radio and put it on the bar counter. There was interest enough to stop the friendly darts match being played. Someone quipped it was like the war; he could remember his dad saying he always had to be quiet for the news, Winston Churchill and Tommy Handley.

'Police are treating as suspicious the discovery of a young woman's body found in a country gateway near the village of Reed St Clements in the county of Lincolnshire. Intensive enquiries are being made in the locality but so far the woman, who is believed to be in her twenties, has not been identified. Speculation that it could be a woman missing from a local hospital would not be commented on. Police say a further statement will be made as soon as progress has been made in identifying the woman.'

'So what about Hoskins?' Buddy's voice rang out across the now-crowded bar. 'He's still missing. I'm going to tell the police about him. It's not right. He wouldn't just go off like that without telling somebody.'

John's objections to an overt police presence could clearly no longer be sustained, and he raised his voice to support Buddy. 'Good idea – they can keep an eye out for him while they're making their enquiries about the murder.'

The landlord's opinion was obviously respected, heads were nodded in agreement and at the word 'murder' from his lips, the banter cooled.

There was another run of orders at the bar and the subjects became more fragmented. A card school started in one corner, and as John had so often observed in the past, it wasn't long before life began to return to normal. He had seen not just tea made and drunk, but meals prepared and eaten in households where he would have thought nothing would ever be normal again. People clung to routine.

The routine of last orders came and went, but it was not until after closing time, and Paul had left, that John began the serious waiting time. He watched the television news bulletins, and the murder was featured on every one. Austin had kept his word about blanket cover by the media.

He pulled the photograph of Liz bound and gagged from his wallet, pored over it, searching for any clue he might have missed then, head on arms, agonized over it. Was it just because he was so tired that every time he closed his eyes his mind kept superimposing the body slumped at the base of a tree trunk? Time and again he lost the photograph to the new picture etched on his memory.

He woke from a first sleep with his neck stiff and hot with pain from its angle on the kitchen table. He woke with his eyes on a level with the photograph and wondered afresh where the hell she was being held. It surely could not be many miles away. A thought occurred; something he could do.

He fetched pencil, paper and ruler, and carefully extrapolated from the photograph all the lines from the tiny amount of background he could see. The proportions of the steps going up above Liz's head were, as he thought, the old-fashioned kind of permanent ladder/steps up to a loft in a barn. He sought out a magnifying glass and learned a little more: the floor was old brick but laid in a herringbone pattern, hours, perhaps weeks, of work done when labour was plentiful and cheap. Paul often featured old barns and properties in his paintings, and he was a local man – he might have a few ideas what or where such a place might be.

He went over the sketch again, darker lines where he was sure of the layout, lighter where he guessed, and underneath a painstaking drawing of the brick pattern on the floor.

His neck and shoulders were so painful when he had finished he had difficulty straightening. He ached from head to toe and knew he had to stretch out, lie down, take his clothes off for a bit, to be in anyway fit to deal with the next day.

He allowed himself a brandy and went to the bedroom, to their bed. He sat on the edge, took his shoes off, not looking at the expanse of emptiness, resolved just to ease his cramped muscles, expecting to have to discipline himself to stay on the bed. Instead he woke with the feeling that he had not moved for many hours, and for a minute remained motionless, praying his waking reality was only a lingering nightmare.

Then he rolled out on to the side of the bed and held his head on his hands, peering at the clock. Six.

Normally he might have gone for a dawn run, watch the light come, put man in perspective with the universe – but this man was never going to be in any kind of perspective without his woman. So instead of running he did her work. He cleaned, vacuumed carpets, spray-polished the neglected bar tables, wiped the kitchen down, checked the fridge, then lost all incentive as he thought of doing the lunchtime menus, a job he and Liz always did together.

He listened to the radio but there was no further news about the identification of the murdered woman. 'Police are continuing and widening their investigations.'

The time crawled to lunchtime, and he opened. Paul arrived at five past twelve, as did an elderly couple for a drink and early lunch. Paul toyed with a pint on one side of the bar, John with a glass of diet coke on the other, just waiting. The couple had ordered lasagne and salad, so no problem there, with ready bagged salads, pasta dishes individually frozen ready to microwave, ditto garlic bread.

When John came back with their meal, Paul had served three workmen with pints and packets of crisps. He began to look very much at home behind The Trap's counter, and while he was there John gave him the sketch of the work he had done from the photograph. 'I wondered if it was worth you having a look at this, being from the area.'

'Sure,' he said, startled when he realized what it was. 'Oh, I see what you're getting at – the stairs – the floor ...' He stopped pushing it into his pocket as more crisps were demanded. 'Doesn't suggest anywhere straight off, but I'll study it,' he promised, 'and I've got quite a few local reference books at home.'

At 12.30 there was some commotion at the front door. They were both instantly alert, ready for any kind of action, but what came through was a large portfolio and a collapsible easel, followed by a large man.

'Good morning,' he said. Only Paul answered. 'I'm wondering if you can help me.' He seemed to address the bar at large. 'I'm on holiday and looking for somewhere to stay while I make a few sketches in the neighbourhood.' Then he looked directly at John as if he had never seen him before in his life. 'I've been told you don't let rooms, but I understand there is an artist in the area who lives alone and might put me up – a fellow spirit, as it were.' He laughed and everyone on the customers' side of the bar switched off.

CHAPTER 9

'I BELIEVE YOU phoned,' John said, staying what looked like Paul's immediate retreat. 'This is the chap you want,' he went on, indicating Paul, who now caught on. 'Things afoot then?' he asked.

'Right.' Austin beamed, appraising his fellow artist with approval, and ordering two steaks with fries and salad for himself and his prospective landlord.

John grilled and ate a steak himself after serving the two men. He had felt suddenly ravenous, and consumed the steak standing, cutting off great forkfuls on every visit to the kitchen for desserts and coffees for earlier guests. For Austin to be here meant a lot had happened at higher levels. Metropolitan detective inspectors do not slip off the duty hook to investigate on behalf of a friend in another force's area.

He took a cup of coffee to the counter and watched as Paul and Austin sat talking, finishing their meal, Austin in his extrovert role as artist, Paul, the real artist, quiet, noncommittal, watchful. Then Austin rose, appropriated another table, and proceeded to open his portfolio. He smiled around at the remaining diners as if inviting all and sundry to look. As the brightly coloured abstracts emerged and Austin declared he thought he had 'found his style', people drank up and left, leaving the bar to the three of them.

John walked from behind the bar and Austin, with little more than a straightening of the shoulders and loss of the rather loose wrist display of 'his' work, became the real man, grasping his old boss's hand.

'Sorry for all that, but we don't want any whisper that there's a man from the Met around. This way—' He hoisted the easel into the air '—I can be out and about without anyone asking questions.'

Paul swore, adding, 'Whatever else you are, you ought to be a thespian.'

'You should have seen his Widow Hanky-Panky in the police panto,' John said.

'But what I don't understand is, if you two worked together and these villains recognized John here, why they won't recognize you?'

John remembered the lanky student his sergeant had resembled, and the lower profile Austin had at that time. 'No chance,' he replied. 'He's got shoulders now.'

'Rugby football,' Austin said briefly. 'But fifteen minutes to closing time, then our cars must leave for your home,' he said to Paul. 'Meantime I wondered if you would act as watchman.'

Once satisfied Paul was stationed in the porch, Austin went back to his portfolio and from a zipped pocket pulled out a slim red cardboard folder with two bold black words on the front: 'Race Case.' If there had been a momentary lightening of the atmosphere, it was gone now.

'The Race Case,' John read. 'Please God, no!'

Austin opened the folder and pulled out two photofits. 'These came through from Paris,' he said.

'Yes.' He certified the men who had eaten at the same table they now used, pinioning them beneath his fingers. 'But...?'

'It's known sections of the original Race Case organization is being regenerated in Paris and London,' Austin said, 'different laundering system, different goods, with arms and explosives as well as drugs in the pot. We also now know the original organization had two groups of hired assassins.'

'And we ...'

'Caught one,' Austin finished for him. 'This—' He too fingered the photofits '—is the other.'

His mouth and lips felt they had a querulous life of their own, but he had to be absolutely clear what he was dealing with here. 'They did not come here after me and Liz?'

Austin shook his head. 'No, you, I'm sure, were coincidental.'

'Just a complication they've ...'

'Dealt with by kidnapping Liz, stilling your mouth until their job is done.'

John looked sharply at him, but Austin shook his head. 'No, that we don't know. We have to assume there's an important contract out, and it must be someone they feel needs dealing with before they begin operations – and the London end is ready.'

'So someone who knows too much, someone they no longer trust,' John contributed. 'But the scale of operations you're describing hardly fits in with our discovery of empty boxes and cases at Creighton Hall. That's more the action of a little middleman.' He paused, remembering the new suitcases, the expensive attaché case. 'Though perhaps not too little.'

'Avarice, I find, works at all levels. Greedy people are greedy in little ways as well as big. They can be setting up paper companies, offshore scams ...'

'But they still like handling the readies,' John finished for him.

'Yes, it gives them a sense of security. Honest folk have policies to cover disasters, our villains like something that doesn't involve a claim form.'

'So if someone has brought dirty money here to hide ...'

'And is recovering it ready to run, this would make him the target.' Austin paused and looked down at the red file. 'Information coming in from the Middle East suggests a political input on the arms front, so all the tubs in this high-risk, high-profit laundry have to be guaranteed waterproof.'

'But does the fact that Creighton Hall was broken into suggest someone else found the cache?'

Posing the question reminded John that they had taken part in many such suggestion and counter-suggestion sessions in his days as Austin's superior, batting ideas back and forth. 'Presumably,' he added, 'if you hide things in a house, you have access, the keys.'

'Own it, you mean?'

'It's a huge old place,' John said. 'That would certainly take us back into the big league, as would a handful of property pamphlets such as this pair had.' He sighed, sat down suddenly. 'So where have we got to?'

'We have a pair of professional killers after a man who's seriously blotted his copy book.' Austin paused to tap the pictures. 'And if they were around when you arrived at Creighton Hall, it's possible they followed you to that garden centre and decided to abduct Liz.'

'Yes,' he agreed, stricken by the thought that he'd let her go off on her own, sacrificed her for the sake of a dozen African violets abandoned on a rubbish bin.

Austin came to put a hand on John's shoulder, then patted his back in that timeless comforting gesture, when words are not adequate. He also took the opportunity to divert John with news about the murdered girl. 'You won't have heard, but the murder weapon was found at the scene. The girl was in fact lying on it. The photographs make it look as if she flung herself at her attacker in her last minutes.'

'That's exactly how it looked,' he confirmed. 'What was it?'

'A large old spanner, of the kind that hung in a set in my grandfather's garage, which only his chauffeur was ever allowed to touch.'

John did not answer. Austin's upmarket background had the source of much private mickey-taking in the force.

'Often,' he went on, 'spanners like that had the name of the car manufacturer cast in the metal. This one had "Riley" on it – only see them in classic car auctions these days. Plenty of blood and tissue, of course, but no fingerprints,' Austin went on. 'Meanwhile

I've sent a man round to Tracey Starmer's flat to get her finger-prints, and DNA, plus the name of her dentist. These may be the only way of proving whether the murdered girl is Tracey or not.'

'The ring tattoo?' he queried.

Austin shook his head. 'The pathologist's report says the hands had been deliberately mutilated. But from her age and size my feeling is …'

'That it is,' John guessed. 'So how does it all tie up?'

'Ah!' Austin took in a deep breath, exhaled slowly. 'The men holding Liz are on a tidying-up mission for some very big dealers. Those dealers are pushing up to the biggest leagues to maintain their nice extravagant lifestyles. They don't want any hostile fins circling their yachts, or storms in their lagoons. That much I would say we know for certain.'

'And do we see the man with the Porsche, the man who picked up Tracey from here …'

'As the man with the big price on his head?'

'He fits the bill,' John said, 'but who the hell is he?'

There was a noise from the front door and Paul came into the bar, pointing to his watch. It was closing time.

'We shouldn't linger,' Austin said, 'but has this local poacher shown up? Can we rule him out of the picture?'

'No, and if it wasn't for everything else I'd be worried sick about the old fellow,' Paul contributed.

They related what they knew of the strange disappearance of The Trap's best customer.

'We'll follow up with another public announcement. The police are on the ground anyway, but you have the hardest part to play – watch, wait, and show nothing. Just have that phone with you wherever you go.'

John nodded.

'And don't do anything independently minded.'

'Or fucking stupid,' Paul added.

John stood on his front step and watched them go, then locked up. For the first time since living there, he felt it was well named. He felt trapped. He prowled around, doing nothing, achieving nothing. The restlessness increased until he found himself in the dining area, fists clenched, hating the smug looks on the faces of some of the pottery ducks. He knew if he did not get out into air and space, he might well do something he would afterwards bitterly regret.

He pulled on tracksuit and trainers, zipped new and old mobiles into his jogger bottoms, locked up and ran.

He did not head off in any one of his usual directions but climbed the fence at the back of The Trap car park and ran out into the country regardless of the fact there were no footpaths, no ways or tracks to follow.

He did not build up to a run as he normally did, he just ran with no rhythm, no conservation of energy, just as haphazardly and uncoordinated as the thoughts tumbling through his mind.

He kept moving until he came to a stout fence separating the fields from a section of the coastal path. He leaned over the fence, laid his head on his hands. He did not realize he was weeping until tears trailed hot through his fingers, but now he let the grief come in great shuddering sobs that shook his whole body, until his chest ached with heaving. He let his hands slide from the fence, doubled over, crouched. No use anyone saying you didn't die of a broken heart; he could feel it happening to him.

His police career had been over when he had avenged himself on those who had hurt Liz before; her life and his would be over if he failed her this time.

He pulled himself back to his feet and climbed the fence, going on. He reached a point where a great bank had been raised leading to the coastal defences further north. When the tide was in these huge silted banks, many over ten metres high, almost disappeared under the water. Here in season came holidaymakers with boats, who went off fishing or cruising, watching the tides carefully so they could get back to their moorings. Some of the boats were still here, at the moment high but certainly not dry, as they lay at angles in the mud slopes, their sides and bottoms green slimed and muddied by the winter weather and their owners' seasonal neglect.

He looked around, not quite sure where he was, but felt a sudden urgency to be back home, on hand, watching and waiting. Over to the right he could see the square tower of a village church. Reed St Thomas. He could go into the village, past the church, circle back to the crossroads – he should be back at The Trap in half an hour.

He had run no more than five or six minutes when he stopped on one of the higher parts of the path. From here he could see pretty much the whole of the layout of the surrounding area, though it wasn't the view that brought him to a standstill.

He could see the low white building renamed Smugglers' Haunt Hotel and nearby a crowd had collected – a crowd in February in Lincolnshire was seven or eight people. Whatever was engaging their interest must have been fascinating for they seemed to be gathered on the very edge of a deep water course. Some, in fact, were venturing some way down.

Then with a pang of alarm he thought of Hoskins. Were those anxious people, and anxious they must be to risk the treacherous mud ravine, even now looking down at the body of the old poacher, caught up perhaps in some net or trap that had dragged him down? With a sense of foreboding, he sprinted the last hundred yards to join the crowd.

One or two recognized and greeted him, made way for him to see. It was both a shock and a relief to find that what they were staring at was a car, but not the elusive Porsche or Rover – this was a green Ford, what the brochures called a Forest Green Focus, that lay longways and well down in the channel. He nodded as previous conclusions were tried on him as newcomer to the scene.

'Not just gone in,' one judged.

'Ah! Been a few tides over that,' a tiny old man said, nodding to

John, who recognized him as a regular darts team supporter, father of one of the visiting players.

'No one in it, is there?' John asked, but unless they were lying right down in the well of the car – or someone had been put in the boot – he could see for himself it was a rhetorical question.

'No one alive, that's for certain.'

'Reckon if anyone tries to get down there, there might be trouble. Need ropes and proper tackle for that job.'

'A crane,' someone pronounced and there was a general murmur of approval.

'I've phoned the police,' the darts supporter said, fumbling between walking stick and pocket to show a mobile phone.

'When did that go in then?' John asked him.

'Not more than a week or two. Don't take long for seawater to rust things up.'

'Pity the number plates are not showing,' John said.

'I suppose,' the man replied, 'but I can make a good guess *where* it went in.'

'Really?' He was interested – and it made an excuse to leave. 'Would you show me?'

'Sure, come on.'

John walked along with him from grassy path, to track, to road, until they came to where the highway ran right alongside the waterway, and to where there was a small extra semi-circle of tarmac, probably put down as a passing place if large vehicles met.

'Look.' He pointed to where the grass on the water's edge was beginning to re-establish itself after being gouged and scraped away. 'I reckon someone tried to turn here. Full tide and that car would go well under. Lucky they didn't go in with it, I'd say.'

'A stranger, in the dark, perhaps,' he said, his brain and his breath speeding up as he calculated the distance from here to The Trap, and from the damaged verge to where the car now lay.

'Perhaps,' the old boy said, 'or perhaps one of the local boyos joyriding in someone else's car, then dumping it, as a change from setting fire to it.' They stood in silence for a moment or two, then he asked, 'Think I've sussed it out right?'

'Yes, I do,' John told him, his thoughts with the state of the girl, of Tracey Starmer, the night Hoskins had found her. Then there was the appalling state of the murdered girl, who seemed likely to be Tracey – nothing accidental about any of that.

The old man beamed at him. 'Think us old 'uns know nothing, most folk.'

'Stand you a pint for being right,' John told him, 'when you're next in.'

'Week on Tuesday,' he was told.

They parted company and he ran on until he was sure he was out of hearing, then took the mobile used only for Austin and pressed the number. He was answered in seconds. It took him a little longer to explain the car, the links he was making with Tracey Starmer, because of where the Ford was and the tides.

It took Austin no time at all to assess and agree with him. Like most policemen he was not a great believer in coincidences. 'I must be on hand when they pull the car out,' he said. 'Leave it to me.'

'Right,' John said. 'And …'

'Paul will be in tonight. I'll see you tomorrow,' he said and rang off.

'Right,' John repeated to himself.

Paul did come in, but Friday evenings were always busy, and before long he was in his now normal role of barman. The bar was abuzz and agog with all the local happenings.

'It was on the radio tonight. "Local waterside dweller, Alan Bernard Hoskins, missing," it said. Anyone with information to contact the police immediately, and a search is being organized.'

They heard Buddy's voice raised above the throng. 'We've offered to help, it being the weekend. They're going to let us know. We've got to listen to local radio.'

'Things moving then,' John endorsed.

'Ah!' someone called from a far table. 'And have you heard about the car in forty-foot drain?'

The centre of interest and the conversation switched from counter to far corner, and John was thankful, just wondering, as he had many times before, how quickly stories spread in the countryside. Liz always said it was like jungle drums.

CHAPTER 10

THE FIRST LIGHT of morning was ruled thin and pale along the horizon, under-lighting and exaggerating the scale of the gantry. It made the car hanging from the crane look like a toy, something you might have pulled from a pile of liquorice torpedoes in a slot machine. Water ran in a steady stream from under the door frames and drained sluggishly from beneath engine and boot.

Austin judged that the boot of the car was weighted with more than just water. It hung heavy, making him feel the lifting tackle should have been slightly more to the rear of the vehicle to make it stable. He knew it was routine, this pause to stabilize the load before swinging it over on to the low loader, but he was impatient and wanted on with the job before sightseers rolled out of bed. More importantly he wanted it all out of the way before John turned up on an early-morning run. Whatever might be found in the boot of this car could then be revealed to him more delicately, more circumspectly – if need be.

He looked over to where Inspector Helen Moore was officially directing operations. She saw his glance and came over to him, pulling up her collar. They had met the evening before, by appointment, as she walked her dog on the beach near Paul's home, and she had impressed him. She had common sense with none of the affectations he still half expected from all women, because that was how his extrovert mother and sisters behaved. One other thing had impressed him: she had quoted Shakespeare. Striding towards him while her springer spaniel was entranced by every wave, she had called, '"Are we well met?"'

'Aye,' he'd replied, '"and here is a marvellous convenient place for our rehearsal."' Both had smiled but left *A Midsummer Night's Dream* there, aware the subsequent lines discussed a killing.

Her approach now was more prosaic. 'We'll be away before the tide turns, or any of the locals are up,' she said.

'Not quite,' he answered. Beneath the suspended car he nodded towards a figure, running, looking as if he approached through a veil of rain as the car still dripped steadily. By way of early introduction he added, 'John Cannon, the man whose partner ...'

'Ah. So we'll hope all normal sightseers stay away for a bit longer.'

They lost sight of the approaching figure as the car landed on the low loader with a thud and an extra slosh of displaced water. At his side the inspector exclaimed in surprise and annoyance. Her upward gesture drew his attention to where John Cannon stood above them. He must have sprinted the last hundred metres, then vaulted up on to the low loader. He walked around the front of the rescued Ford Focus to the driver's side.

'The keys are still in the ignition,' he called down to them, and before either of them could raise even a verbal objection he had opened the door, ignoring another minor rush of water from the interior. Head and shoulders inside, he glanced over into the back seats, then he turned to struggle with the keys in the ignition.

Austin found himself hoping it would be impossible to remove them, that his ex-boss would be forced to allow proper police procedure to take over. But he saw John fall back a little as the keys came free, then he was out of the car, keys in hand, stepping over the slack chains to reach the boot.

'Is that wise?' Austin shouted. 'Let me, let us ...'

'It's a question of my sanity more than your—' he had the keys in the boot and struggled again '—perogative.'

'If you break the key in the lock you'll have longer to wait,' Helen Moore warned.

'You reckon?' he said, struggling on.

Her more authoritarian objection and threat of charges were lost as the boot lock yielded and John raised the lid.

Eerily the wind dropped, or so it seemed, and every breath was held, as John Cannon slowly lowered his eyes then leaned forward into the boot.

'Don't touch anything in there,' Helen Moore warned automatically as John came to the edge of the loader platform and reached a hand down for Austin.

'It's all right,' he said, and once Austin was up there he reached down for Inspector Moore.

All three looked into the boot. At first glance it appeared to have been wall-papered with A4. Individual sheets were stuck at all angles on the sides and roof of the boot, while the main stacks of paperwork had begun pulping into blocks as if ready for recycling. Under some of this random redecoration was a desk computer, tower, printer, monitor, a laptop, and a plastic container, the lid of which had come partly open. From this spilled out keys, sets of house keys – big houses if all the keys on each ring belonged to one property. Austin looped up a set on the end of a pen. There was a tag but the inked address was unreadable. 'All looks like the stuff an estate agent would have in his office,' he said.

The inspector had gone to peer more closely into the back seatwell. 'There's a bag, could be a woman's handbag, under the silt in one corner. But I think we must leave this now to the proper boys. They'll find far more than we ever can.'

'There's a lot for the scientific squad to work on.' Austin leaned closer, and used the pen handle to lift the corner of a bundle of papers. 'Though these,' he said, 'look like estate agent pamphlets. There's obviously a picture at the top and then details underneath.'

'Like the ones I was shown in my bar.' John straightened as he spoke. 'There has to be links between the two—' He hesitated for a second over the word '—assassins and this car ... and ...' He broke off then added with quiet emphasis, 'Or with the bugger in the Porsche who's watching us through binoculars.' They turned to follow his gaze to where, just catching the sun's first rays, there were the unmistakable twin circles of binocular lenses. Then a windscreen glinted and they made out the unmistakable lines of a Porsche, drawn in tight behind a mass of scrub and dried reeds.

'Get on your radio,' he ordered as he dropped from the low loader. Using the vehicle as cover he ran to a screening hedge and a track leading inland. Austin realized he was attempting to get to the Porsche before the driver knew he'd been seen. Inspector Moore spoke rapidly into the mike on her collar. 'No registration, but a Porsche – we have police cars on the main road ready to escort our low loader, alert them. No, not observation.' She looked at Austin for confirmation, who nodded. She continued, 'Stop him, round him up, bring him in!'

Austin swore as somewhere in the near distance a siren wailed. 'What are your lot playing at?' He went on swearing in words loud and Saxon as they saw the Porsche beginning to reverse away, then the driver swing round and drive away inland with the full-throttled roar of a car that would not be easily caught.

The reports that came over the inspector's radio confirmed as much, for not one of the police cars on any of the approach roads had seen the Porsche – though the patrol cars had practically collided head on. This hardly seemed believable, until John came back, looking completely exhausted. He stooped, holding his knees while he found enough breath to explain.

'He's driven straight through a gate, cut across the fields. If he makes it I reckon he should come out on the King's Lynn – Holbeach road, but there's a good many minor turns off.' He paused to suck air into his straining lungs. 'Bring him in, Austin.'

Austin nodded. The orders had already been given.

*

'When shall we three meet again?' The quotation came to Austin's mind as, with all the lights put out in the public rooms, he followed Paul and John into The Trap's kitchen. Not Macbeth's dark witches, or warlocks, but certainly to discuss evil.

He had agreed with John that with so many police all over the area the fact that Paul's car remained late or even all night on the pub car park could be disregarded as a risk. John made coffee, and the other two sat at the table ordering their thoughts like men before a board meeting; a life-or-death board meeting, Austin reminded himself. His eyes followed John Cannon, and pity threatened to invade professional judgement. The man had aged ten years in as many days, and he looked as if he was neither eating nor sleeping. The trouble was, however Austin reasoned the facts, the probabilities, and the improbabilities, his conclusion was that Liz's chance of surviving was hairline.

He let out a long controlled sigh and turned to watch Paul, who had brought back John's sketch of the brickwork, and had other papers looking like printouts from websites, which he was arranging before him.

John brought the coffees to the table, sat down and looked to Austin.

'Yes,' he said, accepting chairmanship. 'Inspector Helen Moore has passed on the information that the murdered girl is Tracey Starmer, and ...' He paused as John shook his head, regretting the girl's death. 'And,' he went on, 'the handbag found in the back of the recovered car is hers.'

'So we can assume that the night she was found and we brought her here – that is,' John's voice hardened as he went on with emphasis, 'when Liz, Hoskins and I brought her here, was the night her car went into the dyke.'

'So you're the only one of that trio ...' Paul began then stopped. He added lamely, 'I hadn't thought of that.'

'And Tracey Starmer has to be the London connection with our man in the Porsche,' Austin continued.

'And he must be the link with the assassins – their target – unless your lot know different,' John said. It came out like an accusation, and he banged his coffee mug down so hard the drink sloshed over.

Austin shook his head and said with measured mildness, 'You know all I know, John.'

'So …' He re-marshalled his composure. 'We have a girl from London's back streets who for years had to work hard to keep body and soul together, in Jimmy Choo boots that I understand would have cost a small fortune.'

'Plus a grudge against the police,' Austin added.

'I see,' Paul said, 'so we take it this Tracey Starmer drove here to help this wealthy bloke. He's used her in the same way these "boyfriends" do who trick women into carrying drugs and bombs and stuff on to planes?'

'Yep! But in spite of her Sat Nav she got lost,' John said, pushing his coffee mug around in circles in his spilt drink, stopping the mug mid-puddle, 'and tried to turn.'

'So when she does meet her friend—' Paul paused to grimace '— she has to confess she's …'

'Lost the lot – papers, keys, computers, everything he was presumably desperate to get out of the capital,' Austin added.

'And also leaving a girl too frightened to even admit she's conscious?' Paul queried.

'She was right to be,' John said quietly, remembering the desperate sprawl of her body.

They had a mutual half-minute silent requiem for Tracey.

Austin re-inaugurated proceedings. 'And so actions as regards tracing this man, we've hundreds of officers over the Greater London area, and beyond, checking on owners of black Porsches. We are widening the search to include places from which it would be possible to drive daily into the city to work. If necessary,' he said grimly, 'we'll cover the whole country.'

'And nothing on the Rover,' John stated.

'Copies of the pictures we had from Paris should have been seen by everyone involved, with orders to concentrate on the men not the car. I feel they've changed vehicles. They can't hide and fulfil their contract ...'

'And release Liz,' John added the quiet wish.

Paul cleared his throat and began to make his contribution. 'I've had a proper look at the photograph—' He slid the copy John had given him from his papers '—under a really strong magnifying glass and this—' He pointed to the floor beneath Liz's bound feet '—is not decorative brickwork, it's very old tiling.'

He now covered the picture with printouts from websites. 'This tiling,' he said, 'is quite distinctive, it's almost unique as far as I know in that it's more rectangular than square, and comes, I'm sure, from a local tile maker operating about two hundred years ago. The company sold over a limited area in East Anglia and look ...' He displayed pages on which were reproductions of patterned tiles. 'Unlike a lot of tiles these were not painted with designs and glazed, patterns were actually incised into the clay before baking. The one unfortunate thing – and the thing that made you think they were bricks, John – is that they were not good in the glazing department. Their glazes did not last – well, not hundreds of years they didn't. But—' And now he pulled out an enlargement of part of the photo which showed only one of Liz's feet and the tiles. 'Sorry about this, John, I couldn't do it any other way.'

Both men now came from their seats and looked over his shoulders as he pointed to what both had taken as random wear marks, the ravages of boots, tools, cart wheels, but Paul traced a fingernail along the lines. 'Look.' He pulled out a pen and applied the etched pattern from the website printout over the marks on the floor shown in the photo, and before their eyes the pattern emerged.

'Do you think there might be records of where these men sold these tiles locally?' Austin asked.

'I have phoned and emailed some of the museum sites, but if I've had no reply by morning I thought I'd go over to Norwich Library in person. That's our best local resource.'

'This may be of vital importance,' Austin said. 'I think we can speed matters up a bit more than that.'

In minutes he was speaking to Helen Moore. She sent a patrol car to the head of the library services, who in turn contacted the head of local history studies, who phoned forty-five minutes later to say he could be at the library by 1.30 a.m.'

'I feel a bit of a fool,' Paul said. 'It never occurred to me that this was possible. I suppose I'm so used to opening hours and ...'

'Being a good law-abiding citizen,' Austin was saying when John announced, 'I'm going to close the pub.'

'It is closed,' Paul reminded him.

'I'm going to close until this is over.'

'I thought we had to keep it open, make things look normal,' Paul protested. 'I could come and live in. Austin could drive my car to and from my place ...'

Austin dropped a hand on Paul's shoulder. He knew John Cannon had reached the end of the time for pretence, of round-about, divisive ways of trying to deal with his trauma. He had seen him reach Calvary before, knew the signs. The waiting, observing the rules game was over.

'No,' John snapped back. 'No! I'll not open this pub again until Liz is here in this kitchen, and if that never happens, then this pub never opens again, not under my ownership.'

Austin felt Paul prepare to argue, but stopped him with a more urgent squeeze of the shoulder. 'You'll need to put up a notice,' he told his friend.

They watched as John found a black marker from the dresser drawer and from the top a sheet of white card. Without hesitation he printed 'Closed Owing to Family Bereavement' and left to pin it on the front door.

'I can't believe this is right,' Paul said.

'The odds are that the hitmen are going to be too busy hunting their target and avoiding the extra police presence to worry about this pub being closed. And time's not on our side – or Liz's. John needs to be completely free to—'

'Follow his quest,' Paul finished.

Austin nodded it was the right word, for it was difficult to predict whether or not John Cannon would survive if Liz did not. Austin thought it unlikely. He would certainly never be the same man again.

As he walked into the kitchen, Cannon stated, 'We left the force to avoid this kind of situation,' then added a peremptory, 'Let's go.'

Austin's mobile rang as they were walking from Paul's car up the steps of the central city complex, The Forum, that held Norwich's library facilities.

One moment he had been diverted by the sight of a fox strolling from the direction of St Peter Mancroft church as if it too was intent on visiting The Forum, the next he was snatched back into the business of police management as dictated by his head office.

Phone to ear, he stopped walking as the implication of what he was hearing sank in.

John and Paul were already halfway up the steps, and he saw them turn to wait for him. He turned away to listen more intently, the news making him throw out a hand as if to ward off what he did not wish to hear. Then his chief inspector, Don Lovett, added an extra bit of information at which he laughed briefly, and dismissed from his mind. He pushed the phone into his pocket and found John had walked back down to him.

'You've been recalled,' John stated.

Austin nodded but climbed to join Paul who was already at the doors being greeted by the senior archivist. He was a tall, thin, professorial man, pale as parchment, but he was immediately galvanized by the credentials of the officer from the Met. Austin pressed the urgency of their mission, never mentioned life or death, but it was there, and the librarian immediately regretted that his own staff were not on hand to make the searches quicker.

At first it seemed slow, but once the archivist had consulted his catalogues and set the system in motion a supply of tomes, ledgers and vellum scrolls were soon on the tables before them.

Austin had decided he would return to London by train, the first one left Norwich just after five. He ordered a taxi for twenty minutes to five, and when the time came for him to leave John walked with him towards the exit.

'The phone call,' Austin said. 'One of our undercover boys has been pulled out of the Thames. We may have to go in quicker than we wanted to, pick up those we're sure of, or they'll all slip away again, relocate again.'

'So, the feeling is,' John said, 'that the London end is more important than whoever these hitmen are after here. In fact, if they're after a flea off their own back, best to let them do the job.'

Austin left the hard logic of this unchallenged and, nodding back to the inner sanctums of the library, added, 'Whatever you find here let me know, and contact Helen Moore – she's au fait with the whole situation. She's your help on the ground, John.'

John gritted his teeth to stop himself saying, 'But it should be you.' What Inspector Moore did not know was him personally, or Liz, or all that had happened before they came to this retreat. Retreat! Ha! That was a laugh.

'She has seen the photo of Liz, she understands the importance of these tiles.'

'So Liz's abduction is—'

'Known to all those who can help. Come on, John, you know the system.'

He just smiled coldly. He had reached the point beyond legal niceties, beyond where any system in the world mattered, and his old friend knew it.

'John, for all—'

'What were you going to say, Austin? For all I hold dear?'

Outside the huge glass atrium a taxi drew up. 'I'll be back as soon as I'm able and I'll phone as soon as I know any more,' Austin said. 'There should be a lead on the Porsche soon.' They walked to the door and Austin turned to say, 'I'm glad you've got Paul,' and held out a hand, but the men suddenly gripped forearms, like gladiators both to be engaged in the same conflict, but at different ends of the arena.

It was 5.30 when the breakthrough came, with details of a man named Cust who had set up a local brick- and tile-making business in 1760. The old business ledgers produced a sales list from 1770 for 'our new tyles', and as if to prove beyond doubt Laurence Cust was their man, in the margins were drawings of the incised patterns.

It was Paul's rapid but meticulous skills in tracing the old maps and placing them over present-day ones that allowed them to make some sense of the old tile maker's records. There were five large properties within a radius of fifty miles they could identify for certain. 'Enough to be getting on with,' John said, taking the list from beneath Paul's fingers.

'There could be more,' Paul said, his hands spread beyond the range of the maps he had copied.

'Yes,' he agreed, 'but it could just as easily be one of these – and I'm going to look at them. If you drop me at the pub I'll pick my own car up.'

'Don't you think we need help?' Paul asked as he drove away from Norwich. 'Shouldn't we let the police deal with it?'

'Don't worry, they'll already know.' There was a hard edge of cynicism in his voice. 'Austin will have already spoken to the library, and to Inspector Helen Moore, probably several times by now.'

Silence fell between the two men; the irritation of hunger and complete exhaustion had surfaced in the exchange.

'We're neither of us fit to go on as we are,' Paul ventured as he drew into The Trap car park once more.

'God knows I can't ask you to do any more....'

'Not until we've eaten, and rested up,' Paul said.

John did not answer, his mind on the revolver he wanted to collect, and he was wondering if he should arm Paul with the second revolver he had secured for Liz years ago. 'Have you any experience of firearms?' he asked.

'No!' Paul said. 'And don't want any thanks. Saw a man shot in the head in South America, brains all over the place – that was enough for me.'

'Right.' He led the way towards the back door. He chose to walk the long way round, to see his notice was still in place, and then through the arched entrance to check the old stables.

CHAPTER 11

JOHN STOPPED AS he and Paul reached the middle of the old cobbled yard, the back of his neck prickling. There had been a sound other than their footsteps, a shuffle, a movement. He spun round to see a figure lurching from the darkness of the old tack room, slumping against the doorframe, then the man raised one hand and something caught the light.

The thought flashed through John's mind that if it was a gun he was left-handed. Then, as if the gesture was too much, the man crumpled to his knees.

'It's Hoskins,' Paul gasped and was on his knees by him, but he was already trying to get up again. 'Why, man!' Paul exclaimed. 'Where have you been? What's happened to you?'

John was by him now, for a second still saw a stranger, the growth of beard, the pallor, the haunted look in the eyes of a man whose reputation was fearless maverick.

Hoskins shook his head as if Paul's question was too big, too much. Then he held up his left arm again – from the wrist hung a pair of handcuffs of the heavy old kind policemen used to have chromium plated to keep from going rusty.

Paul took hold of the swaying cuff, as if in pity, as if concealing it in his own hand might help.

'Let's get you inside,' John said. 'Can you walk if we help you?'

Supporting him on either side they managed, propping him in doorways while doors were unlocked, with Hoskins assuring them he was all right, he'd just walked a long way. 'Where from?' John asked but the awkwardness of manoeuvring him through doorways did not allow for question and answer.

Handling, manhandling, him along the passage to the kitchen, John realized his clothes were in contrast to his appearance. They were clean and dry; not pressed but then his clothes never were.

'Have you been home and changed?' he asked once he was settled into the wooden carver chair by the table.

'You don't miss much,' Hoskins answered but his voice broke as he added, 'I were wet through, thought she might be at my cottage.'

He could see agitation threatening to overwhelm the old poacher, and hurried to pour him a brandy to give him time. 'Who did you think would be at your cottage?'

'Tracey,' he said.

'Tracey?' John repeated the name in disbelief. 'Tracey ... the girl we found out in the lane?'

Hoskins nodded, letting his head stay on his chest, his bottom lip pouted like a child before weeping. 'She was a good gel to me and I'd told her if she got the chance to get to my cottage and hide, told her a place no one would find, but ...' He looked up, a gasp of tears in his voice. 'He's murdered her, hasn't he?'

It was not a question and neither man answered.

'He came back on his own, and there were blood on his shirt cuffs and his shoes. I think it were yesterday, I lost track of time, but made me determined to get away. He spent hours washing ...'

'But did you have any idea where you were?' John asked, anxious to get the vital pieces of information first. 'Where have you just come from?'

Hoskins nodded. 'Allus knew.' He gave a humph of disgust. 'Allus knew.'

John reflected that even in the most aggravating, extreme circumstances, people never changed, but he held his breath and his impatience and waited.

'Handcuffed to a pipe in old Taylor's flat, that's where I were.'

'Taylor?'

'He was handyman-cum-chauffeur at Coupledyke for years.'

'Coupledyke?' John prompted.

'Aye,' Hoskins confirmed.

'Coupledyke House, it's an old place, used to be a rectory,' Paul supplied. 'I thought it'd been knocked down.'

'No.' Hoskins was scornful. 'You can't see it from any road, but it's there all right among a great clump of trees.'

'Built where two dykes met, about a couple of miles from here,' Paul added.

'No more than a mile if you follow the right dyke,' Hoskins put in.

'But how did you ...' John indicated the handcuffs, both ends still locked.

'Clamped me to a great old water pipe. Ruined my knife,' Hoskins replied, and John pictured the businesslike knife Hoskins always carried, a knife that had serious blades, including one like a hacksaw.

'They didn't go through your pockets then,' Paul said.

'Not deep enough.'

John nodded, understanding; poacher's pockets were notoriously deep, often well below the knee. 'So who is the man?' he asked.

'The same bugger who got hold of me near East Salt Marsh.'

'The man with the Porsche,' Cannon confirmed. 'I must talk to Austin at once,' then to Hoskins, 'Hold on a minute – Paul'll get you another brandy.'

'Where's Liz?' he heard Hoskins ask as he went through to the uncleaned beer-stale bar to talk in private.

Austin answered his phone abruptly, and anticipated a mound of questions he clearly hadn't the freedom to answer. He informed John that the local police were taking in discreet searches of all properties the archivist had come up with. If there was any activity at all near any empty properties, observation only was to be maintained until instructed.

'Are you with someone?' John asked.

'Yes,' Austin confirmed, and went on, hardly drawing breath, 'Properties that are occupied are being contacted by the museum on the pretext of wanting to make a more detailed search for Mr Cust's tiles, then plain-clothes men will go in with a museum representative.'

'OK,' John said, aware he could have no influence – and he was going to make his own searches anyway. 'You'll let me know ...'

'Everything, old boy, everything.'

'News from this end,' he said quickly because he sensed Austin was about to clear the call. He went on to tell him of Hoskins' return and what they had learned so far, 'But he's obviously got a lot more to tell.'

'So he's seen this man. Could you get a good description from him right away? We must get a police artist out.'

'Paul's here, he could—'

'Get him to make a start,' Austin cut in. 'Send me a copy over the phone as soon as possible. Right.'

'Right,' John agreed, but felt there was a serious undertone to this conversation he did not understand.

Austin was obviously aware of the unspoken questions. 'Look, old boy, we've got the most unexpected lead on the Porsche owner. Any description from this man Hoskins would be a tremendous help.' There was a pause then Austin added, 'You can take it as certain that this man is the target for our hitmen.'

'So shall I contact Inspector Moore about Hoskins?' he asked, wondering what exactly he was not being told.

'That would be good. I'll speak to her, of course, when I've ... been fully *briefed* by the hierarchy.' In the background he heard someone clear his throat.

The emphasis on the 'briefed' was not lost on him, but as Austin closed the call he had no idea what the significance of this could be either.

He rang Helen Moore before he returned to the kitchen, where Paul had found and microwaved bacon and was putting the cooked slices between bread.

'I've told Alan that Liz is still away,' he said.

'Thanks, good.' He approved the sparseness of the truth. At that moment he needed Hoskins able to concentrate on remembering every detail of his captor's appearance. 'We've got an urgent job to do.' He told them of Austin's request, and Hoskins was all eagerness 'if it helps to catch the bastard'. Paul went to get sketching materials from his car.

'Alan, I want you to show me where this Coupledyke House is exactly. I've got some maps.'

Once more the maps were fetched from the dresser drawer and as John located The Trap, Hoskins quickly traced the line of a dyke from a point near his cottage across country towards a spinney, behind which was a tiny black square John had never noticed before. The horny forefinger tapped this place. 'Coupledyke House,' he said. 'Tiger Taylor lived and worked there for years.'

'So if I went by car?' John posed the question and Hoskins' finger was immediately back on the map. 'You'd go this way, past my place, then turn right here. It's an old way, grown over to no more than a track, but you'd get a car down there, I reckon. Must be the way he used.'

Paul came back and laid sketchpad, pencils, rubber and inks on the table. 'Old maps show a proper road,' he commented, 'but once the Parish of Coupledyke was amalgamated and the rectory empty it became disused.'

John began to appreciate how the Porsche driver could be here, there and everywhere, then just seem to disappear. 'I'll leave you two to get on.'

'Where are you going?' Paul demanded as he hovered near the doorway.

'Upstairs,' he said, and as he went heard Paul begin to question Hoskins – how tall, age, build – so he had a framework of information before they began to reconstruct the man's face.

He went quickly to his and Liz's bedroom, to the metal box bolted into the built-in closet. He took out the larger of two wrapped bundles and from its cloths unwrapped his revolver and slipped it into his trouser waistband.

In the kitchen Paul was asking Hoskins why he thought he'd been taken prisoner.

'He grabbed me first one morning about a week ago. Showed me Tracey's picture in the paper, asked me if I was the Alan Hoskins who'd rescued this girl. Then wanted me to get in his car and take him to exactly where I'd found her. I reckoned he was one of these journalists, told him to bugger off. He got nasty and so did I. A few days later I saw his Porsche near the pub, so I didn't go in. I went straight home and bugger me if he wasn't waiting – with Tracey. I told her a lot of folk were looking for her and she should get herself to the nearest police station. Then he pulled out a gun.'

John felt justified with the decision to arm himself, and the weight and chill of the gun at his side felt less.

Paul was working over the likeness all the time the old man talked, with Hoskins tapping a thick-nailed forefinger to emphasize some aspect or scoring the paper with a fingernail to correct a line.

'The police are on their way,' he told Hoskins, 'and the doctor.' Then turning to Paul he said, 'I'm going to have a look round.'

'A look round!' Paul exclaimed. 'Where?'

'Just around.' He caught Hoskins' eye, saw the old man did not need to ask where he was going. He paused to study the face emerging on the paper. The eyes had received the most attention up to now, and already evoked an emotional response. 'Ah, cruel dark eyes he's got,' Hoskins said softly, 'you've got them right. That's him!'

Cannon wanted off, but stopped long enough to send Austin a shot of the sketch so far. Then he wagged the phone in Paul's direction. 'I'll phone if I need to let you know anything.'

'You're a fool,' Paul told him, shaking his head but at the same time seeing the futility of any objections. 'Just don't come back with any more of these things.' He touched the handcuffs. 'We're not starting a collection.'

'Inspector Moore's bringing an old pair they have at the station. The key from those will fit – one key opened all handcuffs in the good old days.'

'Aye, I remember,' Hoskins said.

'Do you?' John nodded acceptance of the poacher's claim, and left.

He slowed as he reached the point Hoskins had indicated on the map, and even so nearly drove past the old side road. He must have gone by this turn hundreds of times and never noticed it. It looked no more than an entrance to a field that had lost its gate. He turned in, driving very slowly, and could see that at some time tarmac had been laid, but so long ago that grass had grown along the middle, leaving side ruts like an old-time cart track.

Ahead he could see a dark mass of trees, the sky above lighter by contrast. He drove cautiously and as the afternoon faded really needed his headlights but did not want to forewarn anyone. Whoever was in this place he wanted, wanted for Tracey Starmer, for Hoskins, for whatever lead he could give. He wanted that man with all the desperate hunger of a hound starved and ready for hunting.

When he was sure the trees he could see must be the spinney marked on the map, with Coupledyke House on the far side, he looked for the first opening into a field, turned in and parked close under the hedge. He double-checked his phone was on vibration only. Hunter mode, Austin called such preparations, watches synchronized, plans made, eventualities allowed for.

He began to jog towards the edge of the spinney, aware an official report might say he had a heavily blinkered mindset. 'Whatever,' he muttered, just wishing he did not have two people in his head, one of whom was an ex-copper always waiting to write a report on the other.

The late afternoon was not silent for there was quite a wind and as the trees, mostly conifers, closed in around him the wind whined and soughed through the branches. He would have liked to run faster, keep warmer, but dare not, afraid he might come across someone suddenly, or make too much noise – and he did seem to be making a lot of noise. He peered down where his feet fell, expecting to see dry twigs from the trees but the roadway, as far as he could see, looked reasonably clear.

He stopped, stood listening – sounds like twigs breaking under someone's feet went on, and on. He froze but the sounds did not seem to be coming nearer or going away. Then he lifted his head, gauging the exact direction of the wind through the trees – and immediately caught the smell of smoke. He ran faster, wanted clear of these dark trees, still telling himself it could be just a bonfire, a farm labourer hedging, a gardener tidying up.

The trees were much denser here and he realized that what he had thought was just contrast between black woods and sky as he drove along the old road was in fact a light source, which was becoming brighter every second.

He began to get glimpses of an old gabled house lit by bursts of flames. He broke through the trees, and was confronted by the set of a horror film – the Bates family residence. Steep gothic gables were illuminated by spasmodic upsurges of flame breaking from the ground-floor windows, which had already blown out, and from the front doorway where the door had either been left open or burned away.

He reached for his phone, asked for fire and police, gave them as good a map reference as he could, then started across over-grown lawns for what he realized was going to be his first and last look at Coupledyke House.

The fire on the ground floor was too extensive to have started in one place. It looked as if some malicious, calculating mind had begun the blaze at all four corners of the building, and he had reached it just as the four conflagrations met and surged upwards.

Even as he folded his phone, the first-floor windows shattered like a staggered military salvo. Arm shielding his eyes, he watched as the panes fell, the shards and splinters reflecting the flames like a broken misplaced sunset.

The flames might have taken time to gain a hold and meet on the ground floor, but the first floor took no time at all. The fire leapt from the window cavities, lapped up the outside, rolling out, engulfing – and the heat now forced him even further back.

Then with a tremendous woof, a noise like the cry of a myriad animal legions sensing victory, the first floor fell in. He felt it like a blow to his stomach. Before he could release his held breath, the second floor followed, then the gables of the roof tipped and sank. Now there were sparks, now the flames rose higher, higher, until he thought they must be twice the height of the original house. It was awesome – and had it been intended as Hoskins' funeral pyre?

Still shielding his eyes, he moved along what was fast becoming just the shell of the original building, and began scanning the trees lining the old gardens, looking for any movement between the trunks. Fires in these kinds of places were usually the work of vandals, squatters, arsonists – or in this particular case a murderer – and every fire-raiser was fascinated by the results of their actions. He had long ago realized that a perpetrator's compulsion to go back to view the scene of a crime was no myth.

As he reached the furthest extent of the main house, he could see a lesser building that was so far burning only at one end. This must be the old stable block, and garages over which Hoskins had been kept prisoner, where Tracey had spent her last days, not bound or chained, but certainly just as much a prisoner.

John ran now. Was there anyone else in that flat? Was more than just evidence being destroyed?

An outside stairway had been built up to the first floor, undoubtedly to give access to the flat. He sprinted up, shouting, falling into a narrow hallway as he hurled his weight at the door that was not fastened. The surge of heat that met him told him this could ignite any time – and the more doors he opened the greater the risk. But he had to be sure there was no one else here. He shouted again and again as he went in and out of the lounge, bedroom, bathroom, closing the doors behind himself, registering that this place had certainly been lived in and not by anyone as menial as a chauffeur. He raced from room to room but the most hurried glance at the huge flat-screen televisions, the luxurious fixtures and fittings spoke of top quality, no expense spared. Someone had made themselves very comfortable indeed in this hideaway.

Finally he came to the kitchen. Here things were different because it was not smoke he smelt as he opened the door, but steam. It looked exactly as if the carpet tiles had been set to simmer in shallow water; some were actually lifting as the water bubbled.

What was delaying the fire in this room, in this whole block, was a thick old gauge pipe gushing water – the pipe Hoskins must have been handcuffed to, the one he had sawn through.

Even so, he knew he should get out. Even this amount of water was not going to delay things for many more minutes. He wished he could just pick up some clue, something that might have DNA or fingerprints, a brush, comb or toothbrush from the bathroom, a towel, but he could see nothing. He opened the bedroom door, pulled out drawers, opened the built-in wardrobe – whoever had been living here had certainly moved out. Then with what felt like last minute inspiration he threw back the duvet and pulled the bottom sheet from the bed, bundling it under his arm. There was an increased sound of water spluttering as the fire began to win the battle of the kitchen floor. He made for the stairs, the sheet impeding, almost pitching him headlong down.

When he reached the bottom there was a tremendous roar and he knew the upstairs flat would soon be no more – but there was one more thing he needed to do.

He ran to the big doors of the garages and tried to open them but they were locked. He kicked and flung himself at them but to no avail. He ran to the far end, hoping there might be a window. There was.

He was just in time to see the interior lit by a trickle of flame as it ran down from the flat above to a dusty stack of timber in one corner, then rush across the floor like a fuse to its dynamite. It illuminated the trail of fuel that had been laid down to lead to the car. He just had time to register that the car was a Porsche.

He hurled himself down tight to the outer wall, covering his head with his hands and the sheet he still clutched. He felt the vibration of the exploded fuel tank through the ground, heard what he thought must have been the window plus the frame land some distance beyond him. Then things, pieces of brickwork, began to tumble around and on him.

For what seemed like an eternity the ground shook. He could hear for a time – seconds maybe – but was never sure whether in the shifts of bricks, the roar and mayhem of fire, the pounding of his heart, he could also hear a siren.

CHAPTER 12

USTIN ENTERED HIS apartment, leaned back on the closed door, and murmured, 'Ah! Sweet, brief solitude.'

Things were escalating at both ends of the investigation: one dead in London, one in the Queen Elizabeth Hospital, King's Lynn.

When one of their own was found dead, like every force, the Met pulled out all their resources. The result could be over-manning and too much emotion, particularly when some unfortunate had to go and break the news to his wife. There had also been the delicate matter of not wanting to announce the recovery of the man's body. This had been found by a yachtsman well beyond the Thames estuary, and at this point the police desperately needed their quarry to think things were going their way, that the body had conveniently disappeared.

The last report by that undercover officer, whose throat had been cut before he was put in the water, had been that the location of one man was holding up the gang's operations, but that he had only ever heard the mystery man referred to as 'the Dry Cleaner'. The nickname suggested a mark of respect from his fellow villains for a skilled operator, and one who apparently never risked getting his hands wet in the money-laundering business. Austin wondered if this was also characteristic of a man who would use a young girl to transport his papers, computers and keys in the boot of a car to some hidey-hole, then viciously murder her when she got it wrong.

He snapped on all the lights to dispel the images, the memory of the pathologist's unofficial comments of 'no half measures' and 'mincemeat', as he described Tracey Starmer's injuries. The nature of the murder, but most of all the information Don Lovett had first muted and Austin had added to in the last eight hours, he still had difficulty accepting.

If the man the new evidence pointed to *was* involved, then, while he could be regarded as a celebrity in his own field, the press would make him the best-known man in the country. So Austin had to be sure, and all he felt now was doubt. No, he corrected himself, what he felt was incredulity. But he must order his mind, put facts and speculations in their proper place – and wait for his visitor.

He ought to be on the way to see this man at his place of employment, but in view of this particular place of work and the questions he wished to ask he had felt this hardly appropriate. He had instead played on his own father's reputation and invited him to his home. He knew John Cannon would not have approved of this type of old boys networking, but John Cannon was still unconscious, found buried under debris. 'At Coupledyke House – for God's sake,' Austin grumbled at the improbability of the name, as unbelievable as was unpalatable the fact that John and Liz were now – he paused for the right words – 'both in jeopardy'.

John Cannon's presence at the scene of Hoskins' imprisonment had not gone down well. The surge of anger at the man's stupidity was stilled when it was learned Cannon had only been found by chance – by the sighting of what a fireman had thought might be a white garment under rubble – and that he had been got out only just before a massive explosion had completely wrecked the garage block, and brought down the huge gable end next to it.

Paul Jefferson had been devastated by the news and was in constant touch with the hospital. Austin had arranged with Inspector Moore that John should have a constant police presence, officially justifiable by the fact that if and when he came round he might be able to give them some vital lead. More importantly, as far as Austin was concerned, it would assure that his friend and mentor stayed put.

Meantime Paul had finished the artist's impression of Hoskins' captor and according to the old man himself it was 'wonderful, and no police drawer could do better'. A copy of this likeness was now in front of Austin, together with a newspaper facsimile of a court artist's impression of a case at the Old Bailey that had hit the headlines towards the end of the previous year.

Austin knew he, and come to that his senior officer, had been guilty of procrastination. He had delayed investigating the name of a particular black Porsche owner – until Paul's sketch had come through. Even then he had judged it a coincidental likeness; after all, court artists tended to exaggerate features, to dramatize. He looked at the drawings, tried the nickname, 'the Dry Cleaner' and judged it a preposterous idea, but after the arrival of Paul's sketch he could no longer ignore the links to this man.

He glanced at his watch: five minutes to the appointed time. He would be surprised if the man he waited for was even a minute late.

He had been more than shocked to find that Mr Parmar was in fact still clerk to the barristers in the Chambers where his father had practised, and retired from, as head of Chambers. He remembered the little Indian with his brilliant black eyes with some awe, for his father had always shown a kind of intimidation, linked to total respect, for the man who controlled his Chambers. A small man, he ordered his barristers, most twice his height, with a gracious manner, but was, according to Austin's father, exemplar of the saying 'an iron hand in a velvet glove.'

Austin permitted himself a small whisky and water as he waited, aligned Paul's drawing on the table beside the bottle of single malt and placed a crystal glass ready for his guest. His desk clock flicked its figures over to six. Austin was turning down his lips in disappointment when the bell rang.

He pressed the release on the outer door, turned the newspaper facsimile face down, and went to meet his guest at his own front door, smiling at the neat, brisk figure that came rapidly up the stairs. Age it seemed had not so far wearied Mr Parmar – it wouldn't dare.

Their handshake, mutually and unselfconsciously, involved all four hands as Austin drew Mahendra Parmar inside, amid a dozen comments and enquiries.

'Austin, how's your revered father?'

'Good to see you, Mr Parmar, thank you for coming.'

'The pleasure is mine.' His beaming smile made the pleasantry true.

Austin took his coat and led him to the lounge, held up the empty glass and filled it until Mr Parmar gave him the nod. 'You remember my vices too, I see.'

'So what can I do for you?' Mr Parmar asked as he was directed to the best easy chair. Austin handed him the likeness Paul had made. 'Aah!' Mr Parmar seemed to acknowledge full understanding of his own question.

'You know him?'

'This is why I am here, surely?'

'This is an artist's impression of a man we are anxious to talk to.'

'It is a very good likeness of one of my barristers.'

'And does that man own a black Porsche?'

Mr Parmar nodded repeatedly. 'He does,' he said then looked directly into Austin's eyes and stated, 'This then is a tactful, but official, enquiry.'

Austin nodded.

'Of a serious nature.'

'As serious as it can get,' Austin said and watched Mahendra Parmar very closely indeed. The little Indian sat motionless and silent while the desk clock flicked over a full two minutes. Austin was prepared to wait much longer.

'So, he has reached the end of his rope,' Mr Parmar at last reflected.

Austin thought it was an odd phrase to use in the circumstances, but he recognized, with a growing sense of excitement, Mr Parmar's lack of outrage at the idea that one of his own might be involved in a serious police investigation.

'The ... incidents,' he said, 'would involve this man being away from the City for quite a while, particularly in the last few weeks.'

'That—' Mr Parmar thought deeply before finishing his sentence '—with this gentleman is always entirely possible.'

'It is?'

'Austin, I need to know more, before I speak about one of my barristers, even this one.'

'Even this one?'

Mr Parmar made no reply and no movement, waiting now as Austin had waited for him.

He told the story, acknowledged Mr Parmar's concern when he heard about John Cannon, who he had met, and his abducted partner, and finished with the enquiries in London about owners of black Porsches that had at first concentrated in the areas near where Tracey Starmer had lived and worked. Then the area had been widened. 'This was when—' he paused to indicate the sketch Mr Parmar still held '—it included a barrister making his name in criminal prosecutions and working in my father's old Chambers, and I delayed – in fact, I laughed,' Austin admitted. 'Took other names first, but when this artist's impression came and I found this ...' He now turned over the paper with the court artist's impression. 'I knew I had to contact you.'

'I appreciate you did not come to Chambers on such an errand.' Mahendra Parmar sat shaking his head, eyes shuttered as if privately reviewing all he'd been told. At last he looked back at his host. 'Have you a picture of the murdered girl?'

The question surprised Austin, but he rose, went to his desk and drew out copies of a snapshot of Tracey Starmer supplied by her neighbour and the picture from the Lincolnshire newspaper.

'This is not the girl he brought to introduce to head of Chambers at our Christmas party.'

'So he ...' He paused

'Mr Gerald St John Gyatt.' Mr Parmar supplied the name they had both so far skirted around.

'... is not a married man. Isn't that unusual by the time they come to be top barristers?'

'Not so much in these times.' Mr Parmar tutted. 'But Mr Gyatt knows it would do his standing no harm at all if he had a partner, preferably a member of the aristocracy such as the honourable lady he escorted to the Chambers Christmas celebrations. I think Mr Gyatt sees himself as Sir Gerald St John Gyatt, or even Lord ...'

'So unlikely to take up with a working girl,' Austin said.

Mr Parmar uttered a low word in a language Austin did not know, then rose suddenly and began to walk around the room, his tutting like the sound of an old clock, so regular was it. 'No, I think this has to be said,' he declared as if in response to some inner debate.

'Mr Gyatt is an ambitious man,' he declared. 'No, he is a greedy man.' He resumed his chair, but put his hand over his glass as Austin approached with the decanter. 'My tongue is loose enough,' he said. 'I would not say this to anyone but you, Austin, but Mr Gyatt is the only man I have ever had in Chambers who I have come to like less and less the more I am acquainted with him and his ways. He wants only the big money briefs.'

'And you say he could easily have been out of Chambers?'

Mr Parmar nodded. 'He has always been a barrister who wants to know what briefs he is being allocated as early as possible. Once he knows his immediate commitments he spends little time in Chambers. He is in touch, but always takes his work away with him. I have to use his mobile telephone number if I need him at other times. He likes at least half a day's notice if he's wanted. That can cause some trouble with head of Chambers.'

'We have his home address as Streetly West, well south of Newmarket,' Austin said but did not add that he had already looked at the map and thought the roads to Norwich and King's Lynn were pretty direct from there.

Mr Parmar nodded. 'He employs a full-time secretary-cum-housekeeper there to help look after his aged mother. I understand it is the old family home.'

'I need to contact this man immediately.' Austin felt he need mince his words no longer. 'Because he is either a murderer, or he's a damned annoying red herring,' Austin said.

'You sounded like your father then,' he said. 'What can I do to help?'

'Would it be possible for you to call him now and ask him to come to see you in the morning?'

'It would, but my Chambers ...'

For the first time Mr Parmar showed the diffidence Austin had expected much earlier in this conversation. 'We will be tactful. If we get this wrong you can imagine the furore it would cause, the press ...'

'To say nothing of the judiciary, and I could hardly be on your side if that happened,' Mr Parmar said, 'but I could phone him to say I have a brief he might be interested in.'

Austin keyed in the code to make the call untraceable and handed over the phone. Mahendra Parmar tapped in a long number he knew by heart, listened, then frowned. 'His mobile is switched off. I've never known that before.'

'Never?'

The Indian shook his head solemnly. 'Never.'

'And so significant?'

'Or a mishap, a coincidence. Such things do happen.'

'I've already allowed Mr Gyatt a large share of coincidence. I have to go after him.'

CHAPTER 13

I T WAS VERY late when he drove slowly through Streetly West, locating the Gyatts' family residence, which was in darkness. He went on until he found a large hotel on the Newmarket road that had all-night staff and could offer him a room.

The conference with his fellow senior investigating officer, Don Lovett, before he left London had been detailed. Chalk and cheese might have been a just comparison between Austin and Don Lovett. Lovett, whose background, several generations back, was a mining family from Durham, and who was not given overmuch to words, let alone flowery phrases, had done most of the listening as Austin convinced his colleague that if Austin handled all the enquiries linked to the Dry Cleaner and the situation involving a – as far as they knew – live hostage, it would be less amorphous than a single, blanket operation.

'Cannon?' he had enquired, and Austin replied that he was still unconscious in hospital, but not deeply so, and there was brain activity. Lovett had nodded and suggested, 'When he comes round, keep him there.'

Austin slept only fitfully in the hotel bed, and was up, showered and first in to breakfast. Before he left the hotel he rang The Trap, feeling he needed news of John, Paul and Hoskins before he embarked on – at best – a tricky day.

The phone rang for what seemed a long time, and when Paul answered he could tell he had woken the man. 'I didn't call you from the hospital,' Paul said, 'because there's really no change. Hoskins has been interviewed by your people, at length. He wanted to go back to his cottage but the doctor said he should not be alone, and it was either stay with me or go into hospital. The inspector also said he was best to stay here, as there were quite a few press cars trawling the area, waiting to pounce on anything that moves. So far all they've been told is that he has been found safe and well; no one knows where he is. Any news on your front?'

'None I can give you,' he said, 'but progress of a kind. I might be back with you by tonight.'

There was a hesitation at the other end, then Paul asked, 'As yourself, or ...'

'More important than ever we should keep the London connection under wraps.'

'So I'll get you a bed ready here, shall I?'

'Good idea, all under one roof,' Austin endorsed.

After settling his hotel bill, Austin drove back towards Streetly West. He had decided the simplest approach was the best. He drove into the short circular drive before the detached three-storey Victorian house, parked directly in front of the door, ran up the steps, rang the bell and waited. He rang several times and stood listening. Eventually turning to view the neighbourhood, he saw a tall, sprightly lady approaching him up the drive.

'Good morning,' she called. 'Can I help? Karen's gone to her mother's.'

'Good morning to you.' He noted the spare frame, the lightly tanned face of an active outdoor woman in her late sixties. 'It's actually Mr Gerald Gyatt I was hoping to contact. Karen would be ...'

She hesitated for a moment. 'Karen Lane. His housekeeper, I suppose.'

'Not his mother's carer?' he suggested.

'No, no, Karen didn't arrive until after his mother had been taken away.'

Now he did raise his eyebrows at the way this clear-eyed woman phrased the explanation. 'So the house is empty,' he stated.

'Has there been an accident?' she asked with the usual stiffening of the backbone ready for shock.

'Nothing like that, but I do need to know Mr Gyatt's whereabouts.'

'His Chambers ...' she began, but he shook his head. 'Is it about one of his cases?'

'Well ...' He hesitated long enough for her to presume it might be, but he saw her lips tighten. She was not to be easily drawn, and he deemed it time to produce his warrant card if he was going to learn anything more.

She inspected his credentials carefully, appraised him again. 'Inspector, my name's Joan Burnham. You'd better come next door to my house.'

He followed willingly. Early in his police career an old beat constable had told him to listen very carefully to old people, particularly when they were neighbours of suspects. Joan Burnham led him through to the kitchen of her house, and a pleasant, warm place it was. An ancient Aga on one wall, and filling the opposite wall an antique dresser full of warm cream meat plates and tureens. She caught him looking and smiled. 'My people were farmers, couldn't bear to part with all the old things when they sold up, a good many years ago now.' She opened one of the top plates of the Aga and pulled the already-singing kettle over it. 'Tea or coffee?' she asked. 'It's not his mother, is it?'

'No, I've no information about any of Mr Gyatt's family.'

'There is only his mother.' She assembled things for tea.

'Have you been a neighbour of the family for long?' he asked.

'Since before Gerald was born,' she replied. 'We all moved in as newly marrieds. Now I'm on my own, and Gerald just comes and goes.'

'And Karen Lane?'

'For a long time in her eyes, and mine come to that, she was his partner, or she aspired to be.' Mrs Burnham placed teapot and cups in the middle of the table and sat down opposite. 'Though now she's more like caretaker-cum-occasional secretary. He seems to drop in for any letters or messages – bills mostly to do with his mother. Karen says that's all that ever comes. He gives a few orders about what he wants doing in the house and garden et cetera then usually goes off and we don't see him again for weeks, even months.'

'So he's certainly not living here, and if Karen wanted him urgently?' he asked as he sipped the excellently made tea.

'A message to his Chambers, I suppose. It wouldn't do for me,' she said, then laughed. 'How old-fashioned that sounds.'

'His mother is in a residential home?'

'I think it's a bit more than that,' she said.

'A nursing home,' Austin assumed.

'No, more private asylum.'

'So she really was taken away.'

'Yes, but don't draw any wrong conclusions, Inspector. Gerald went to extreme lengths to keep his mother at home, and – in my opinion – she was certifiable when Gerald was a little boy.'

Austin worked at keeping the excitement from his voice: the profile of an abnormal childhood often preceded the maverick adult. 'I'd be interested to know about him as a boy, what kind of life he had.'

'Why?' The question as direct as her eyes.

He held her gaze. 'He could have information about a very large money-laundering operation....'

She exclaimed and leaned back in her chair. 'You mean he could be involved?'

'In his position it hardly seems likely, does it?'

'Money!' The word had all the resonance of a dud coin, and she sat shaking her head, reminding him of Mr Parmar. 'When he was a little boy Gerald stole from me. It began with money I left out for the window cleaner ... but I only once threatened to tell his mother.' She looked up, anguish in her eyes. 'He actually got down on his knees and prayed me not to. Can you imagine this little dark-eyed boy, looking like an imploring cherub, kneeling … They say people steal because they believe life owes them. Well, it owed Gerald.'

'So you didn't say anything?' he asked, wondering if she had done that small boy any favours by keeping quiet.

'I was afraid of what his mother might do; her rages could be quite out of control. I wanted the boy to feel he always had a refuge here, but I made him understand how wrong it was.' She gave an exasperated sigh. 'But he carried on stealing money for years. At its worst it became like a macabre game. He made a point of finding out when I had delivery men – coalmen, milkmen, whoever – coming, and no matter where I concealed the money for them, it would disappear.'

She lifted the teapot towards him and he nodded acceptance of a second cup.

'Gerald was just seven when his father committed suicide, undoubtedly driven to it by his mother. My husband and I used to say that from the moment she conceived Gerald, nothing ever pleased her again. Desperately sad for us when our greatest wish was to have a child.'

'I can imagine,' he murmured.

'Though we're detached we could hear her shouting and smashing things. She was a great thrower – anything that came to hand – plates of food from the table, cutlery, saucepans. Then every weekday morning she began coming to their front door and screaming after her husband, things like, "I'll look after your worthless brat while you go off enjoying yourself."' She paused, shook her head. 'That man worked hard, but he could never please. Everything he ever did was made a mockery of. She sapped his strength, drew the will to live out of him. She was outrageous, out of control. She needed treatment; no one would have believed a quarter of what we heard as neighbours.'

'So as Gerald grew up, he was alone with his mother?'

'Yes, though his father had set up a trust fund for him and he went away to school at eleven,' Joan Burnham said, adding, 'Now that was the best thing he ever did.'

But from seven to eleven, formative years with a mad woman, Austin thought.

'He was a clever boy, brilliant was a word on many of the reports he brought to show me, but I'm afraid it didn't make him popular. He was too intense, too watchful. I always thought his light-fingered ways would get him into trouble either at school or university, but he must have mended his ways.'

Or become very clever at it, Austin thought.

'I mean,' Joan Burnham emphasized, 'to become a man of the law.'

'Indeed, a leading defence lawyer in the criminal courts,' Austin endorsed.

'Yes, I have seen him. I sat in the public gallery at one of his big trials,' she said, but there was no enthusiasm in her voice. 'You know his father was a gentle man, too kind, too sensitive, but in court that day Gerald was so like his mother. The feeling of contained anger as he addressed the jury, the cleverness as he cross-questioned, it was aw … ful.' Her voice fell as she split the word. 'I felt quite mesmerized by his control of the court, his rhetoric. I felt no one would have dared to even suggest he did not have justice on his side.'

'Tell me a little about Karen.' He was wondering if she was the young woman who had impressed at the barristers' Chambers Christmas gathering. 'Does she come from any kind of a monied or aristocratic background?'

She looked at him with gaping-mouthed astonishment. 'What on earth made you think that?'

'The idea of a suitable partner for a barrister, perhaps.'

'Well, then, that'll be another reason why he'll never marry her. She adores her mother, who was unmarried, never knew her father and apparently has no wish to. I've always tried to warn Karen not to expect too much of Gerald, though I believe he's very generous and she's been able to help her mother quite a lot. She goes over to Downham Market once every week since Gerald bought her a car, and now he's given her time off, a proper holiday – the first I remember her having – she's gone for longer.'

'Downham Market,' he repeated, trying to place the town in the triangle of places that was building up in this case. 'Not far from King's Lynn?'

She nodded. 'Money obviously hasn't been a problem for Gerald for years, but I had presumed it was all honestly come by these days.'

'Do you have the mother's address in Downham Market?'

'Yes,' she said but made no attempt to rise.

'There's something else,' he ventured carefully, 'about Gerald – or Karen – something that's worrying you?'

'Something I had not thought about for a long time, but talking of years ago and then thinking about Karen …' She looked up at him as if for help.

'Sometimes little bits of information we have stored in our brains come together and are …'

'Much more meaningful,' she finished for him. 'Yes, that's it, but these are such little things, and so many years apart I can't see how they would help.'

'Just tell me then we can decide.'

'I told you how Gerald went on taking money when he was a young boy, well, he – I can't believe how odd this seems, now I come to say it out loud – he used to draw pictures of the money he'd taken, cut them out, and I'd find them—' She indicated the dresser '—in a drawer or under a piece of crockery, wherever he'd taken the real money from.'

'You tackled him about this?'

'Yes.' All animation had gone from her face. 'It was a terrible moment. He lined up all the paper coins he'd made and asked, "Is it worthless?" It was a word his mother often used: worthless husband, worthless son.'

'And Karen?' he prompted.

'One Easter a couple of years ago I thought Karen was finally going to leave. She was so upset. Gerald had been here for a whole weekend and had actually taken her out, to Newmarket for lunch and shopping. Then Gerald left and I didn't see Karen again for quite a few days. I was sure she was avoiding me, and after that she was never again the young woman who'd waved happily to me before they left for that jaunt. To be honest I'd rather expected her to come back from Newmarket with an engagement ring. I'm sure it was what she expected, and had a right to expect – living in his house, it was high time. Eventually I did mention what I thought, and she scoffed at the very idea – no, laughed bitterly would be a better description. Then she said a strange thing, some-thing like, "Oh no, he wanted me to have something quite worthless – a symbol he said it would be. Well, he knows now that doesn't do for me."' She stopped, tutted. 'Sorry, that's all, it just linked suddenly in my mind to the pictures of the money Gerald used to draw and cut out – you know, not the real thing – worth-less symbols.'

'I understand,' he reassured her. 'These details can be very important.' Feeling he had scooped far more than he had expected, he prepared to take his leave. He impressed on her the importance of letting the police know immediately should Gerald come home at any time.

She nodded. 'But you will remember what I said about life owing Gerald, won't you? I mean, if he is involved in this money-laundering thing....'

'Everything will be taken into consideration.'

'Oh!' She tried to sound light-hearted. 'Policemen do actually say that.'

'I'm rather afraid we do.' He took her hand. 'Thanks for the excellent tea.'

He drove out of sight of the house then phoned Helen Moore and arranged twenty-four-hour watch on Gyatt's home address.

Karen Lane's mother lived in a cul-de-sac on a small estate of semi-detached bungalows on the outskirts of Downham Market.

There was a small, smart car in the drive of number 40, but though he went to both front and back doors he received no answer to his knocking. He noted the tidiness of the end-of-winter garden, snowdrops flowering in the short back border, and the fact that all the windows were closed. He looked over the neatly cut privet hedges but it seemed there was going to be no helpful neighbour voluntarily coming to his aid here, though lights were already on both sides.

These two bungalows were in the occupation of the elderly, who did not have a loving child who visited regularly, the nets and the slightly unkempt state of the front lawns and borders told him this. He knocked loudly at 38, and though he could hear every word of an afternoon chat show he received no answer.

He went to the bungalow on the other side. Here he saw the nets move as he entered the front gate. He knocked and waited, listening to a certain amount of shuffling on the other side of the door. Then it was rather thrown open, and he was confronted by two unsmiling women, undoubtedly sisters. He had the impression of two large, grey, woolly squirrels with black, suspicious eyes.

'Good afternoon, ladies,' he said. 'I am looking for Karen Lane. I believe her mother lives next door.' He indicated number 40 with the parked car.

He thought he caught a concerted low 'hmm', indicating this was exactly what they expected he would be doing, and the pair seemed to consolidate into a tighter bloc. 'She said it was too good to be true,' the rear said and the vanguard nodded bravely, and added, 'If you've come to fetch her back …'

'You can't, she's gone.'

'Gone? Her car's still here,' he said. 'So she's not gone too far, perhaps.'

'Far enough,' the back marker proclaimed.

'Think she's called your bluff this time.' The fore marker took hold of the door and prepared to close it.

'I think you may be mistaking me for someone else,' he said.

'You're the man who employs her at Streetly West.'

'No,' he said, experience telling him that a one-word answer put the onus on the other to keep talking.

'Oh!' The solid front of grey cardigans and skirts relaxed a little. 'Only she said it was too good to be true, a paid holiday with no limit and no conditions, and ...'

'No limit?' he queried.

'She didn't believe it either, so she's took her mother off to Spain for a fortnight. Said he wouldn't be able to fetch her back from there.'

'When did Karen go?' he asked.

'Last Saturday. We're feeding the cat.'

'And she's not left an address – on purpose.'

'Well, thanks very much.' He bowed his head to the two of them. He saw no reason to alarm these two timid, watchful beings with more questions. 'I am so sorry to have disturbed you,' he said.

But it was Austin who felt disturbed as he drove away from Downham Market. Disturbed because he now needed more resources: a man to make enquiries at travel agents to find out where Karen Lane had booked her holiday, possibly someone to fly out to Spain to interview Karen Lane. But if the 'symbol' turned out to be a tattooed wedding band then Gyatt – if they could find him – was 'in deep mire', he said aloud, 'Unless the assassins find him first – then his earthly troubles will be over.' But where did that leave Liz – and Cannon?

He knew before anything else he must drive straight to King's Lynn Hospital.

CHAPTER 14

CANNON FELT HE floated up towards some surface, but heavily
like a sodden timber, with the added sideways push and pull
of deep water. The movement seemed to accelerate, exaggerate, lurching as if even these depths were storm tossed – and
there were lights above the surface that swam and swung in a
nauseating way. He screwed his eyes tighter, feeling he much
preferred to stay wherever he was.

'John?' someone quietly prompted him, and again, 'John?'

He tried to say 'leave me alone' but he heard only a disgruntled
mumble. He tried to go back to whatever darkness had engulfed
him until that moment; it hadn't hurt, it hadn't swum about,
flashed lights or had voices challenging him with names. Then one
name hit him like a physical blow.

'Liz!' he exclaimed, opening his eyes wide, and now the lights
hit him like close lightning as he tried to rise. He was … He tried
to rationalize where he was. He must have had an operation; this
felt like coming round from deep anaesthesia. There had been an
accident, he thought, and he'd been buried – and dug up it seemed.
Or was it resurrected? He tried to laugh.

'John.' The voice reached for him again and something in the
tone made him want to focus on this person whose voice meant
something to him. The lights resolved themselves into overhead
circles and the walls and curtains around him locked into place.
He located the speaker. Austin? Shouldn't he be in London? Now

his memory came back, rushed back in rip tides, full of mental anguish. 'Liz?' he again demanded.

'No news,' Austin said, 'but ...'

The rasping growl of frustration and grief in his throat blotted out the rest of the placatory sentence. He flung out an arm, dismissive, angry, and knocked over a stand, dislodging a plastic drip bag. Then there were official hands, check and dark blue uniforms, trying to override something he had to do.

He gripped Austin's sleeve as they tried to move him from the bedside. Someone moistened his throat with a sip of water, someone else tried reasoning. He gripped tighter. 'The Porsche,' he said, 'went up in the garage – Coupledyke House.'

By the time Austin sat down in the kitchen of The Trap with Paul and the unnaturally pale-looking Hoskins, Paul had already received a call from John Cannon. The sister had taken the telephone trolley to his bed, first telling Paul that he was not allowed more than five minutes. In answer to his enquiry, she replied that yes, he had all his faculties, and was himself – 'That's provided he was a headstrong impatient man before his accident.'

'I was there when he came to,' Austin told them. 'His first word was Liz.'

'He asked me if we'd made any progress tracing the old tiles.'

'And?'

'Nothing ... the police and the museum staff have covered every house in their old records,' Paul said. 'It's wasted a lot of time and caused a lot of trouble. I'm sorry I ever raised the matter.'

'There was a lot of trouble about old tiles a few years back,' Hoskins reminisced.

Paul swore about old tiles in general, but Austin prompted Hoskins. 'What kind of trouble?'

'Oh! It were when some Londoner came to live 'ere. He discovered these tiles in his back kitchen – made the national papers writing about them!' Hoskins' scorn was obvious.

'Weren't they genuine?' Paul asked.

'Well, I suppose,' Hoskins scoffed, 'them things lay about in an old yard for as long as anyone's great-grandparents could remember. Everyone who wanted to repair a wall or a floor went up to Cust's Farm for a cartload.

'Cust's Farm,' Paul repeated. 'Cust's Farm! Where the hell is that?'

'Just a bit of a tumbledown old barn left now. Men like Buddy and them would know about Cust's bricks, and I remember many a muddy gateway being filled in with 'em when I was boy – be well grassed over b'now.'

Paul was clearly mortified by Hoskins' wonderful memory and the whole museum episode, but Austin had another idea. 'Have you seen the photograph of Liz?' he asked.

Paul shook his head. 'I spared him that.'

'With his local knowledge, I think he should.'

'What's this?' the old man asked.

'John was sent a photograph of Liz ...' Austin began.

'He told me she'd been taken.' Hoskins nodded in Paul's direction. 'When her John was in hospital and I couldn't understand why she didn't come home.'

'It's a photograph of Liz – bound and gagged.' Austin warned.

Hoskins took the picture and angled it so the light fell fully on it. 'The bastards!' he whispered. 'The bloody, sodding bastards.'

Both men watched him as he poured over the photograph, holding it this way and that, at length putting it down on the table, his hands clenching into hard knobbly fists.

'Well,' he said at length, 'I think I can tell you where that is.'

'What!' Paul started from his seat. 'What?'

'You really think you can?' Austin asked more circumspectly, calming the other man and gesturing him back to his seat.

'Yes, I know that old set of steps.'

Austin reached over and caught the old man's arm. 'She could still be there,' he said quietly.

'Not ...' Hoskins shook his head. 'Surely not still trussed up like a bloody chicken!'

'Anything you can tell us will help,' Austin urged.

'The steps – can you be that certain?' Paul was still unconvinced. 'There must be hundreds, well, dozens, of such sets of steps in Norfolk. They'd be produced in some workshop somewhere ...'

Hoskins shook his head, his hand hovering over the photo before he delicately tapped the top of the steps above Liz's head. 'These are in an old mill, Stetford Mill, not far away. It was going to be renovated, made into a house. I went to have a look.' He gave Austin a quick glance. 'See if there was anything any good before they started ripping the place apart. I remember those steps because they were just what I could'a done with for my outside loft, but you'd never take them apart, they were too heavy, too well fixed.'

'You're sure about this?' Paul asked.

'Never seen steps set just like that in any other mill round here, and see ...' He peered closely again, the other two with him. 'They're fastened by extended angle irons. As the mill wall circles away, each iron's longer. Take an army of men to shift 'em.'

'So is it a house now?' Austin asked.

'No, the builder who bought it started work, then went bankrupt. Think it's up for sale again.'

'There's a map,' Paul said, heading for the dresser.

'Don't need no map, I can take you there now,' Hoskins offered. 'We'd need lamps – it's a dark old night.'

'We'll need extreme caution,' Austin said. 'These men must not be alarmed, or they may harm ...'

'Kill,' Paul interjected.

'... their hostage.'

Hoskins leaned back in his chair. 'We've had one lass killed,' he said. 'That's enough.'

After a moment's silence Paul added, 'And it's a good thing John's still in hospital.'

Austin fervently hoped he could be kept there, but he had grave doubts though saw no point in wasting time voicing them. 'A map would help, I think, to pinpoint this mill, and I presume—' He looked at Hoskins now '—you can tell us what the surrounding ground and countryside is like in detail.'

Hoskins' forefinger stabbed at the spread map without any hesitation. The other two peered at the spot between river and dyke where a building was marked. 'Ah! I know it,' Paul exclaimed, 'but never knew its name.'

'The waterways look straight as a die,' Austin said.

'You try to walk straight and you'll be floundering in the reeds and mud banks,' Hoskins warned.

Austin ran a finger along the lines of first the river and then the dyke. 'And there are no bridges over these where cars, or anyone come to that, could slip away?' he asked.

Both men now shook their heads.

'Right,' Austin decided, 'I need to know all about this mill and any outbuildings. I want to know how big every door, every window is, whether they can be opened, and if so could a man get in or out? What the layout of the mill is once we get inside? Everything you know – perhaps Paul could do sketches.' Then he phoned Inspector Helen Moore.

She arrived quickly, alone, from home, but other officers would soon join them, she said. The situation explained in full, she looked solemnly at Austin and stated, 'So we have to go in – early morning is usually the best time.'

'In position before it's light,' he added.

Paul made coffee as more officers, a chief inspector and two sergeants arrived, all in dark clothing as if Operation Stetford Mill had already begun.

'We ought to recruit you two on to our permanent staff,' Inspector Moore said, overlooking the growing plan of the mill and area, and the written details, as Paul and Hoskins consulted and worked on them, undeterred by the many different hands and fingers pointing and questioning over their shoulders.

When all were satisfied that they had every last detail, every piece of information out of the two local men, Austin called them all to order.

'So let's sum up.' He indicated that they should spread around the table so they could all see. He tapped first the large-scale Ordnance Survey map. 'So we have here a mill, on which building work was commenced, but was only in the early stages. When Mr Hoskins last visited the area he remembers that the builder had put doors on the garage because he was keeping his materials in there. It's also possible the ground-floor door into the mill may be boarded up.'

'Our battering rams can deal with most barriers anyway,' the sergeant built like he'd be useful on the other end of such a tool commented.

Austin detailed the lay of the land with the help of Hoskins and Paul. 'Our main trouble is going to be getting to the mill in the dark.'

It was Hoskins who grunted agreement with that statement, and suggested, 'Your best chance is to let me take you up the river side, and Paul 'ere lead you up the dyke side – that's straighter.'

'Civilians on a police raid.' The chief inspector shook his head.

'That be buggered for a tale,' Hoskins said. 'I've forgotten more about hereabouts than you'll ever know.'

'Ever walked along a river bank after high tides have forced the waters back and eroded the banks?' Paul asked quietly. 'I'll tell you this, you'll be in the wet and briny with all your fancy equipment.'

'Sir,' Helen Moore addressed the chief inspector, 'this if you remember is Mr Alan Hoskins, the local man who was missing, and who has particular local knowledge....'

'Ah!' He spread his hand over his mouth, recollecting, hiding any expression. 'That Mr Hoskins. So we know we have an expert on moving about in the dark.'

'When we get to the buildings you two must fall back immedi-ately,' Austin said, leaving no time for more nuances and niceties. 'No heroics – you could get in the way, hinder us and cost Liz Makepeace her life.'

Details of roadblocks and armed units were added to the map Paul had made and it quickly took on the appearance of a full battle plan. When every last police officer around that table seemed satisfied there was nothing more that could be done to make this operation as foolproof as possible, the assembly time was fixed for just under three hours' time.

'I could do with my wet-weather gear from my cottage,' Hoskins said.

'Don't worry, we'll kit you out,' Helen Moore promised. 'I'll be back here by two, we'll move out at 2.30 and aim to strike between 3.30 and four. Villains are not usually at their best in the early morning.'

'So when we fall back,' Paul queried, 'what happens then?'

'You two put your heads down and your hands over your ears,' Austin advised. 'It can get wild and noisy.'

'But hopefully for only a few minutes,' Helen Moore added, as her radio came to life and at the same moment Austin's phone jangled. The two sergeants and the chief inspector began pulling on coats ready to leave.

They all stopped to listen as Austin and Helen Moore both exclaimed, 'What!'

'Shite!' Inspector Helen Moore exclaimed, her eyes on Austin, whose frozen, tense demeanour was more eloquent that any tirade of obscenities.

'John Cannon is missing from the hospital,' he said flatly. 'They've searched the hospital and the grounds. No one can remember seeing him since dinner time.'

'But one patient said he was helping to serve from the trolley in his ward,' Helen added.

No one wasted time on the obvious. No one voiced the fact that surely he should not have been out of bed so soon. No one asked what he was doing in another ward serving dinners. They reconvened, standing shoulder to shoulder to adjust their plans.

CHAPTER 15

SOMEWHERE IN THE middle distance a dog barked – once. The noise fell sharp as a blow on Austin's eardrums. He listened intently for any repetition, any frenzy that would alert the whole area to their ambush.

He glanced at his watch: the digits showed 02.56. He judged that even if the dog did raise the neighbourhood every route out of that mill should by now be covered. There should be no escape. all runners, in whatever direction, would be swept into his net – but the bark was not repeated.

He knew Hoskins was by his side, but was quite amazed at the old man's capacity to stay completely still, to negate himself so completely into his surroundings. The perfect poacher, John had called him, and he began to understand why. When the question of seeing in the dark had been raised, Hoskins had just assured them that by the time they'd been out there an hour or so they'd be able to see enough to move about.

The old boy was right. By the time the digits reformed themselves into the hour Austin could make out the fog lying like a blanket to just above their ankles, and while there was no moon, the river seemed to give off its own light.

He stepped towards Hoskins but was startled as he felt a knot of rope pushed into his hand, and the other end was immediately tugged for him to follow. The poacher had obviously made his own judgement and arrangements after listening to the talk of communication restraint and night sights. They moved forward at a slow, steady pace, but even on the end of a guiding rope Austin's feet were soon soaked. He tried to follow the meandering way with Hoskins avoiding places where the river had taken bites from its bank, while he, even on the end of a short rope, kept blundering into them. He wondered how the others were coping without a guide, and decided this was the nearest he ever wanted to get to trying to walk on water.

At that moment he could be convinced a nice town siege with a loudhailer and a mediator was much more civilized than this soaked black countryside. He wished the air held something more piquant than the dank smell of rotting reeds and grasses.

'Rotting in hospital,' had been one of the protests John Cannon had called out to him as Austin left his bedside. By now it was likely he was back home at The Trap. Austin did not envy Paul, left to keep him happy with whatever story he could muster, until this raid was over. Paul had very reluctantly accepted that he was the one who must stay behind. He was the person John would expect to be at The Trap when he made his 'surprise' arrival. Paul had elected to lock up and go to bed once they had all left, to make things appear normal, and to give the operation time to be well underway before John could start asking him awkward questions.

He peered ahead and realized he could actually make out the black figure of Hoskins moving just in front of him, and to the left he could see the shape of an ancient, stunted willow. He glanced to the sky; could see the shape of a moon behind thinning cloud. Too late for any further precautions, and he greeted the moment with dread and excitement, the moment when his stomach churned, when time went from dragging to pulling – when the responsibility for lives was his. He had the authority to call the whole thing off and he had the obligation to push it forward to its bitter end.

He started as Hoskins' hand was suddenly on his chest, then

running down to his hand and taking the rope from it. 'A few more minutes,' he breathed.

Austin glanced at his watch. Hoskins was right again: his watch showed 03.28, two minutes before they stormed in. He could see the old windmill like a great black stump against the paling sky, and the squat bulk of the building Hoskins said was a store place or a garage. It was large enough to hold several cars, and there could be an inside door through to the mill, but of this no one was sure.

He looked down, and saw the lighted figures change from 03.29. to 03.30. 'Go! Go! Go!' he ordered, and for the first time he stepped ahead of Hoskins, his turn to stay the old man where he was. 'Thanks,' he said as he left him and sprinted the remaining fifty yards towards the mill. 'This,' he said through clenched teeth, 'is for you, John Cannon.'

He reached the building at the same moment as the sergeant with the ramming device and two more officers. Their target was the main door into the mill. He saw them try it, then stand back as the sergeant swung in for the first blow. Austin ran to the garage, and could immediately see that one of the doors was not fully closed. He wrenched at it, hard, nearly falling as it came easily towards him.

The mill door had not yet yielded but between the blows he could hear men running in from many directions as he charged into the garage, gun in hand. There was a car parked at the far side – a Rover, he was sure – but he didn't pause, for at the back there was a door through to the mill, and from that partly open doorway a light shone, a dim electric light.

An electric light burning and a Rover car in the garage could only mean the hitmen, the old Race Case assassins, were here.

The passage was narrow and his shoulders bumped the curving walls as he ran until he came to a three-way option. Another passageway made a T-junction to right and left, and there was a closed door straight in front of him. He chose the door and followed the drill: stand to the side, kick in or open – this one opened at the lift of an old latch – then flat to the side wall, then challenge. 'Armed police! The place is surrounded. Come out, hands up!'

No response. Both hands steadying the gun, he stepped into the doorway. He'd done it many times before; the doorways always yawned like chasms as he stepped into space. His gun swung round the empty room. Here too a dim 40-watt bulb was on.

Here were the basics of a kitchen, a table, two chairs, an electric kettle, toaster and cooking ring. On the table were the remains of a meal, beans on toast, partly eaten. Men made themselves such meals but rarely left them less than half finished. A third plate of one slice of toast with beans was not touched, and neither was there any provision for that third person to sit down. It looked like a strange rendition of *Goldilocks and the Three Bears* – who's been eating my beans on toast and where was Goldilocks?

'Where?' he breathed as he paused to listen to the inside of the mill, pushing away the noise of men gaining entrance, the hustle and banging of nearby doors. But beyond, nothing, no panic on this floor, or above or below. He shivered; it felt as if a pall lay over all, and every keen animal instinct he still possessed cried get out, run away, this is a terrible, bad place. He was not allowed such luxuries and turned from the kitchen to urge the men on faster, faster, cover the ground, see all there was to see, whatever horrors, get it over with, let's see and deal, be done with speculation.

There were men with lamps in the passage to the right of the kitchen, and the lights showed a shadowed recess in the wall and steps down. The sergeant and the two men who had battered their way through the door were almost there. 'The stairs,' he said, indicating the alcove. They plunged down and he followed; from dreading what he might see he now wished he were in front as he noted the angle irons from steps to wall. Hoskins was right again.

They were all on each other's heels, the sergeant shouting, challenging, as they reached the spot Austin recognized from the photograph. Here was exactly where Liz had been bound and gagged.

One of the constables held his lamp high, swung it quickly around the circular cellar once, and then again slowly. It was empty: there was absolutely nothing, no furniture, no abandoned rope, nothing. There was no sign now of anyone ever having been kept down there – no immediate sign.

Austin beckoned the man with the lamp to the bottom of the steps, took the light himself and stooped down, casting the beam carefully over the surface. The beam stopped, reduced as he lowered it closer to the floor. He had picked up a bright gleam, a glint, in one of the old incised patterns.

'What is it?' the sergeant asked, stooping beside him.

He pointed to a long blonde hair, then he swung the beam an inch or two either way, and saw others, shorter, scattered.

'This is where they cut off Liz Makepeace's hair,' he told them, 'then sent it to Cannon.'

There was a moment's silence, then the sergeant said, 'We're on the right track then.'

Austin thanked his God for practical men, who could bring his constables – and his superior – back to the job in hand. 'Yes,' he said, 'we'll leave this to the forensic boys.'

As one they turned, climbed quickly back to the ground floor, and then began up the stone steps to the first floor. Above them they could hear men searching, heard the challenges, the pauses, doors thrown back.

They were almost to the first floor when they met an armed officer, gun lowered, coming back towards them.

'You'd better come and have a look, sir.' He nodded back the way he had come, but stood back, letting Austin go first.

This room was dark. Austin lifted the light and could see the narrow window had been blocked with boards and old sacks. Spaced across the floor were long dark mounds, laid out in a row like graves in a churchyard. Five. Not all the same size, but each shape covered with a blanket.

'A bloody massacre,' someone breathed.

'What in God's name?' the practical sergeant cried out.

'The devil's more like,' Austin said as he stepped inside and stooped to the first mound. Picking up the extreme edge of the blanket, he lifted it, cautiously at first, then higher, finally flicking it aside. Underneath was an empty sleeping bag pushed up into a body shape. 'Imagination can make cowards of us all,' he muttered and turned with some relief to the second mound. As the lamps were carried further into the room he could see that a dark corona, a circular stain had seeped from under this blanket.

He lifted this blanket edge with even more delicacy, to reveal a man shot in the head at close range. His whole face was distorted into grotesque surprise by the force of the bullet entrance wound. It was from the back of the head, the explosive exit wound, that so much blood had seeped. Austin recognized him as the taller of the two assassins in the Race Case.

'One of the hitmen,' he said, lowering the blanket gently.

He moved to lift the third blanket – again a kicked-up sleeping bag.

'Some maniac's got a sense of humour,' the sergeant muttered as Austin prepared to lift the fourth cover.

Austin braced himself for the next revelation.

A second body. More time had been taken here, for this man was more formally laid out than the first. The arms had been crossed on his chest and beneath them the jacket and trousers had been pulled straight. This man had been shot twice, in the chest and in the head. He was just as hefty as the first, but not so long, in life not so tall. The face was more obliterated by runs of blood but it had dried in blacker concentrations where it had filled and lain in the many pockmarks on the cheeks.

'This is our second hitman,' Austin said, 'but not shot in here.'

He moved himself delicately back a step or two and pointed to trails of dark colour on the ancient planked floor.

'Shot out here,' the hefty sergeant, still holding the battering ram, called from just outside the room. 'There's blood splashes all over the walls.'

One last mound remained, the smaller one near the window. Two bodies, two sick jokes, so the fifth...? Stooping to the edge of this last blanket, Austin had a sudden picture of John in his hospital bed, appealing, hand outstretched to him as he moved away.

He raised the blanket. There was a concerted release of breath as the fifth mound was another moulded-up sleeping bag. Several men swore softly. Austin felt a tear pain sear his nose. He took his time replacing this last blanket, time to regain control.

'Are forensics on the way?' he demanded. 'Has the whole mill been searched? No sign of the young woman hostage?'

He knew the answers to every question, but it helped to ask, it helped cover his anguish, his anger, frustration and complete surprise at the outcome of this raid. By the time he had stormed around, taking no notice of reassurances of the areas covered, going over the whole place for himself, including the garage and the Rover car, he felt somewhat sorry for those who trailed after him.

Inspector Helen Moore joined him back in the kitchen. Without touching anything, he bent to try to judge how long the beans had stood congealing on the toast.

'Yesterday morning,' she guessed.

'Three plates, two chairs, but three sleeping bags upstairs ... so where is Liz Makepeace now?'

'John Cannon is back at The Trap,' she told him. 'One of our men saw him arrive, and he's still there.'

'So if the target got to and turned the tables on the hitmen, why take Liz? Why not dispose of her at the same time? A clean sweep. If the same man killed Tracey Starmer he's obviously not squeamish about killing a woman....'

'We will have to drag the river and the dyke,' she reminded him.

'Why bother to take her out of here?'

'Right.' She took up his line of thought. 'And how would he take her away? There is only one set of tyre tracks in and out of the garage, and they're the Rover's,' she reported. 'If he walked, or dragged her, I'm afraid it's going to be difficult to tell now.' They both silently reviewed the number of men who had been over the tracks and paths.

'What are you thinking?' she asked.

'I'd like to issue a warrant for the arrest of Gerald Gyatt.'

'You think you have enough evidence to?' She looked doubtful. 'He's an eminent man, and isn't it all a bit circumstantial?'

'Not the links between the Porsche and Tracey Starmer....'

'But you've no identification. A Porsche, yes, but not necessarily Gyatt's Porsche.'

'No,' he admitted, knowing that with Karen Lane as yet still untraced in Spain, and no forensic on Gyatt, plus the fact that the public issuing of a warrant might panic him, push him to dispose of Liz if he hadn't already done so. 'No,' he repeated, 'not yet, but I will get him.'

'I'm sure you will.'

Helen Moore's reply startled him. He had not intended to speak aloud, and his slip made him sharp. 'Surely it shouldn't be too difficult for forensics to identify some part of the Porsche that went up at that Coupledyke House.'

'They haven't yet.'

'Stir them up,' he ordered, 'and there's plenty more to do here. 'I'll be back at The Trap. I have to tell Cannon.'

CHAPTER 16

AUSTIN AND HOSKINS walked into the pub kitchen to confront a standing, aggressive John Cannon – and a seated, defensive Paul Jefferson.

John looked first at Hoskins, who had taken off his coat and was now unlacing his wet boots, then at Austin, and stated, 'Your trousers are soaked. Where have you been?'

'Trying to follow …' He nodded towards Hoskins. 'And failing.'

John looked back to Hoskins, expecting some remark, some skit, some grimace, but there was nothing, no response, no change of expression.

Something like an electric shock shot from the base of John's spine to the top of his head. He sprang to his feet. 'What's been going on? You two out together in the middle of the night, and …' He gestured to the state they were in. 'Have you found something? Liz …'

'No.' Austin's denial was loud, authoritative. 'No, John. We have not found Liz, or any trace of her whereabouts at this moment. We've found where she *was* held – and we've found our two men, our assassins.'

'Found? What does that mean? Found and let escape? Arrested?'

'We found them dead, both shot in the head, one also in the chest.'

That slowed Cannon down. 'So had Liz shot them?' he asked.

Austin shook his head. It was not an option he had considered. He did not, at least not this quickly, want to explain the scenario of the bodies, or his theory that they might not just be dealing with a solitary, greedy man, but with a man whose mind had perhaps gone the same way as his mother's. Instead he repeated the most mundane thing he could think of in such circumstances. 'No weapon's been found as yet, and we're waiting on forensics for quite a few things.'

'So where was she?' John asked. 'Where? I don't even know where you've been.'

He was told where and why as Jane Purdy and Paul began to fry sausages and bacon and cut mounds of bread.

'And you've searched the whole area?' John asked.

'Everywhere, everywhere.' It was Hoskins who spoke with utter weariness.

'And the search of the surrounding area goes on, of course,' Austin added.

'Of course,' John echoed and in the bleakness of his voice was the knowledge of the frogmen and the underwater search team no one was mentioning.

'I'd like us to confer, John,' Austin said.

'You'd better get him some dry trousers,' Hoskins said as the smell of bacon frying filled the kitchen.

'There's joggers in my wardrobe,' John said. 'Underwear on the top shelf.'

The joggers were a little short and the underpants a little snug, but coming back downstairs Austin felt the external and internal man was always better for food and warmth. His mind was quite another matter.

In the bar John had put a match to the fire, brought sandwiches for Austin, and on a table was a roll of the white card he used for pub notices, plus red, green and blue pens.

Previous to John's departure from the Met the two of them had devised a system, not unlike logic studies, a reasoned system of speech bubbles containing facts, or suppositions, which could logically be deduced one from the other. Certainty was always in red, supposition in green, blue for impending actions. To this day Austin always carried pens of that color. He pulled these from his jacket pocket and laid them at the other end of the table.

They exchanged glances over the blank card. 'We'll have it on the wall as we always did,' John said and walking over to the dartboard unhooked it from the large sheet of hardboard and put it aside. Then taking the card he stretched it out, holding it in place with two sets of darts.

He turned to face Austin, who saw the unfortunate image of John's head surrounded by darts, as if he was the target in some missile-throwing act, or St Sebastian about to be martyred by better-aimed arrows.

'Before we start theorizing,' John said, stepping forward, breaking the image, 'what do you think has happened to Liz?'

'Whoever shot the assassins has her.'

'And the person most likely to have shot them?'

'Their target, the man with a very large price on his head.'

'So their target, the target wanted by this new gang now has my ... has Liz to bargain with.'

'Yes,' he said, just wishing he felt the situation could be that easily defined, wishing he didn't keep seeing the five mounds, wishing he didn't know Gyatt's mother was in an asylum.

'She must be nearly out of her mind,' John said quietly.

Startled, it took Austin a couple of seconds to realize John was talking about Liz. 'Perhaps time to put a few facts on the wall,' he suggested.

'I presume Don Lovett's in charge,' John stated.

Austin nodded. 'He's dealing specifically with the London end.'

The bubbles began to blossom across the card, big bubbles filled with red facts. Tracey Starmer's life, and death. The Ford and its contents, lost in the dyke, and recovered.

The Porsche blown up at Coupledyke House in red, and at this point as Austin told of the links to Gerald St John Gyatt QC, green links to Mr Parmar's and Joan Burnham's evidence. 'What we don't want are any mistaken identities.' Austin went to tap the QC's name. 'Particularly not with a chap like this.'

'So in red,' John went on with smaller balloons on lines leading from the recovered car and from the brief lunch the two hitmen had taken at The Trap, 'pamphlets dealing with large house sales, and the names of the two properties Liz reconstructed from the biro marks on Tracey Starmer's hand.'

Like a fierce lecturer he rounded on his seated audience of one. 'So into our sphere from the London case comes Tracey Starmer, a target, two hitmen ...' He paused for a contribution.

'... and a large amount of money in boxes, suitcases, briefcases.'

'Recovered in a hurry, probably by the hitmen who then saw Liz and myself at Creighton Hall, followed us to the garden centre and abducted her from there.'

'That last could go down,' Austin judged, 'in green.'

'Right,' John said and did so. 'But we're running on too fast, we're losing the hard fact of these pamphlets.' He tapped the appropriate circles. 'They turn up twice, and Tracey Starmer has a bootload of stuff.'

'Unfortunately both the desk computer and the laptop were brand new, bought from a computer megastore and paid for in cash, and a lot of A4 was from new packs that had come undone in the water.'

'But even so perhaps some kind of clue in itself ...'

'If he was planning to open a new office, an estate agency,' Austin said, 'but Gyatt's a Queen's Counsel.'

'But what we do know,' Cannon pointed back to the appropriate circle, 'is the assassins had a fistful of pamphlets in this very bar.'

'Do we have any doubt that we're talking about the kind of details you get from an estate agent?' Austin asked.

'No.' John was emphatic. 'But by the time we saw them in here—' He demonstrated the table where he and Liz had served the men '—someone had scanned them into a computer, deleted all details of locations, then reprinted them.'

'Why?'

There was silence in which the coals slipped in the grate and John mused on the obvious. 'Our hitmen thought the information would lead them to their target. By the same token the man with the price on his head deleted them to keep the assassins off his track.'

'Right.' Austin agreed with that.

'So, properties, estate agent leaflets, are the leads to Gyatt wrong? Is he just a red herring?'

Austin remembered asking the same thing of Mr Parmar and recognized John's tone of devil's advocate. He was being pushed to enlarge on his ideas. He frowned. A police officer did not say things like his heart saying one thing and his head another, but looking up at Cannon he caught the merest nod of understanding – and like all cornered things went on the attack. 'If forensics would just come up with something so we could link the Porsche at Coupledyke House with Gyatt....'

'What's taking so long?' John asked.

'Detective Sergeant Maddern has a team of men over there working through the rubble,' Austin told him. 'It surely can't be long before they find the chassis.'

'Then the chassis number has to be traced to a dealer, the dealer to a buyer. Have we got that much time? Has Liz?' John asked, and for a moment his voice broke, but he turned sharply to look at the chart. 'So at this point we know Gyatt is difficult to pin down, but we know he's kept the old family home, not too far away....'

'Streetly West,' Austin supplied. 'I want to contact this girl who's been housekeeping for him, now taken her mother to Spain because Gyatt suddenly gives her proper time off, which was apparently quite unheard of before. I gather the relationship had been more like a live-in partnership until then.'

'Except you say he was hardly ever there.'

CHAPTER 17

THOUGH CANNON TRIED to concentrate on the route and the driving, the area was too well known to him, and all he was gambling on learning at Streetly West too important. He was basically travelling on the basis of a look on Austin's face when he spoke of Gyatt and his home life.

'No, that's not all,' he assured himself, pushing the red sports car along the country lanes. He went over and over exactly what had been planned that morning before Austin and Helen Moore had left The Trap.

Austin and Moore were overseeing the investigation of all high street properties recently let or sold which might be suitable for the business of an estate agent. From existing estate agents, details would be obtained of any really large properties that had passed through their books in the last ten years, and whether or not they recommended any particular firms of solicitors. They were also producing Paul's sketch of Hoskins' abductor and the original photos of the two dead men to see if anyone recognized them.

What was tactfully referred to in John's presence as 'the routine searches', were underway; reserve underwater teams had been called in. Moore had added that now there was no fear of the hitmen being able to do any further harm, the wholesale search of derelict, disused and summer-use-properties was already well underway. She paused to spread her hands in as wide a span as possible over the table, adding, 'And Sergeant Maddern is still searching the ruins of Coupledyke House for identifiable pieces of the Porsche.'

John had done his best not to harry them, understood they were trying to do their official duty and tiptoe around his feelings at the same time. He knew there were other operations to do with the London end of this whole case he could not be told – because he was, after all, just an outsider. Though whether this was how he was going to present himself when he reached Streetly West he very much doubted. He had already deceived Paul when Hoskins had gone on and on about needing to check his cottage. He had suggested Paul could drive him over and be back in half an hour, leaving Paul little alternative but to take the old boy.

'You'll ...' He specified nothing, but John had known his own dishonesty as he nodded reassurance, and had left in the MG in under fifteen minutes.

When he arrived at the street of detached Victorian houses he noted the ubiquitous white Mercedes van at the far end of the road, and knew his car number would be taken as a matter of course. He cruised until he saw The Rowans, the home of Joan Burnham. Next door was the house much grown over with the stems of a Virginia Creeper, bare now, but its leaves would well cover the front of the house before many more weeks had passed. This was the childhood home of Gerald Gyatt QC as Austin had described it.

He parked before The Rowans and walked up the drive and rang the front door bell. Inside he could hear a radio, which increased in volume as if someone had opened a door on the way to answer his summons.

He was surprised when Joan Burnham opened the door. He was expecting an older woman – well, an older-looking woman.

'Good morning,' he said, 'my name's John Cannon, I'm a colleague of Inspector Robert Austin who came to see you the other day.' He was aware that he was deceptively reaching for his inner pocket, but she smiled and asked him in with no question whatsoever.

'I'm quite pleased you've come,' she said.

'Has something happened?' he asked. 'Mr Gyatt? Has he been back to his house?'

'No, no, I told your Inspector Austin that I would let him know immediately if he did.'

'And you would know if he came back?'

'I'd know if he made more than a fleeting visit. I'm not on watch all the time obviously, and I do go swimming every Tuesday and Thursday afternoons, but I can see any lights that come on in the house, and from the front I do overlook his drive.'

'But you seemed concerned.'

'It's just that this morning a parcel came for him, from the nursing home where his mother is.' She gave him a little look to see if he knew what she meant, and he nodded his understanding. 'As far as I know there's never been anything sent like this before, and I'm really not sure whether I should ring his Chambers. I've tried to ring Karen, his housekeeper, you know, but she's away at her mother's, and there's no reply from her mother's house, which is unusual. I've never known that before either.'

'Karen's taken her mother to Spain for two weeks,' he told her, 'having been given a formal holiday period from her employment.'

She gasped. 'Really! Well, good for her.' Then she shrugged and added, 'So Gerald's finally stopped pretending she's any more than an employee.'

He raised his eyebrows quizzically but did not speak.

'I explained a little to Inspector Austin,' she said, ushering him into a pleasant sitting room with French windows overlooking a long garden broken by curving and well-maintained herbaceous borders. 'For a long time Karen hoped for something more permanent than general dogsbody, a very well paid dogsbody, mind,' she emphasized, 'but Gerald doesn't seem to be able to get his relationships right with women at all.'

She paused and smiled at him and as she did so was startled to see his hand cover his mouth as if in alarm. 'Are you all right, Inspector Cannon?'

'Yes, of course.' He smiled back, quite unable to voice what had caused his sudden distraction, what he had just seen. He knew now why this woman had disconcerted him as she opened the door. He forced himself on with another question. 'So Mr Gyatt does not have any lady friends you know of?'

She shook her head slowly. 'I've never known him to have more than an odd date or two with any girl, and that was back in his university days. I certainly never met anyone. It was one of the reasons I thought he might eventually sort himself out and settle down here with Karen.'

'Sort himself out?' he prompted.

She drew in a deep breath. 'Since Inspector Austin came I've thought an awful lot about poor Gerald. I think he can't get his relations with women right because he couldn't come to terms with his own mother, could not deal with her. Perhaps what he never properly realized was that neither could anyone else.' She shook her head. 'His other problem is that he can be like her. I saw it more and more as he got older. He was unpredictable; you couldn't quite get to grips with him. One day I could feel I was really becoming close, and believe me, I tried, Inspector, I tried, then the next day ...' She smiled ruefully. 'Don't they say our genes are half and half, half from our father, half from the mother.'

He nodded confirmation. 'A basis of DNA,' he said, but what he could not confirm was the hope this woman had given him. Whether it was unreasoned hope, last-ditch hope, he was not sure, but it spurred him on to new efforts. 'You did mention a parcel,' he said.

She stood then paused. 'Do you mind if I ask you a question? Inspector Austin obviously thinks Gerald is involved in criminal activities. Does your visit mean that this is more likely than it was before?'

'Yes,' he said unequivocally. He would have liked to have added that after the forensic team had collected DNA samples from the shot men they might well be at Gyatt's house to take samples from there – but this was more than he, in his unofficial status, dared assume.

'I'll get the parcel,' Joan Burnham said, and was back in seconds with a large brown paper parcel. 'In the circumstances I'd be pleased for you to have it,' she said. 'I'm at a loss to know what to do with it anyway.'

He took it, noticing a sender's label stuck bottom left: The Dadd Ward, Kimberley Hospital, Kent. 'A long way to go to visit,' he said, frowning, another thought hovering, but Joan Burnham bridled a little, defensive of her neighbour.

'Gerald took a long time before he found a place he was happy for his mother to go to – a very long time.'

'Do you have a key to his house?' he asked. 'I was wondering if there could be other post?'

She shook her head. 'I suppose it's unusual – good neighbours do, I'm sure, but not the Gyatts.'

He thanked her and left his own mobile phone number – 'just another contact' he explained should there be any news or sighting of Gerald. She hesitated before she opened the front door. 'You know, whatever Gerald's done, he deserves some pity.'

He did not answer.

As he drove away the parcel on the front seat next to him seemed to grow in size, until he could concentrate on nothing else. He stopped the car in the first lay-by he came to. Lifting the parcel on to his knee he calculated the several pounds' worth of stamps it had needed, looked again at the sender's sticker: 'The Dadd Ward'. He remembered that some time ago he had been leaning on his bar counter stuck on a crossword clue: He even remembered the cryptic clue – Pa in a cell painting fairies. Paul had been in and given him the answer, told him of a Richard Dadd who had been an artist and worked for much of his latter years in an asylum after murdering his father – painting fantasies and fairy stories. He felt a shiver of conviction that it was why Gerald Gyatt had chosen to incarcerate his mother there. Gyatt, a barrister who dealt in stated cases to make his legal arguments, would have liked the idea of the Dadd Ward.

He knew he should have opened the parcel carefully so if necessary he could repack it without anyone knowing, but he was well past caring about such niceties. He took his penknife from his pocket and cut through the sellotape and brown paper at one end.

Inside was a tightly folded and packed pile of clothes. They looked like blouses and fine woollen cardigans neatly sealed inside a clear plastic wrapper. He peered into the brown paper again and found an envelope. This was not sealed.

The address at the top of the letter was just as on the parcel and the envelope, to Mr Gerald Gyatt, at his Streetly West address. It seemed that the psychiatrist in charge of Dadd Ward, with the list of letters after his own name, was not aware that his patient's son was probably more distinguished than he was. The tone of the letter suggested neither did he care.

'Dear Mr Gyatt,' the letter read. 'Please find enclosed articles of clothing etc which we found after you had collected your mother on ...'

Collected his mother – did they mean her body? Had she died? He consulted the date – four days ago. The next paragraph answered one question.

'In your interview with my subordinate at that time, I believe it was pointed out to you how difficult it might be to readmit your mother at any future date, should you take her away. I write now to confirm that this is indeed the position.

'Although the Dadd Ward of this hospital has always been a private resource for psychiatric patients, and continues to be so, under new arrangements we now act as an overflow hospital for National Health Service psychiatric patients ...'

In other words they didn't want her back. He turned over the clothes in his hands, the kind of bundle which in his police experience would have gone into the general clothes store used for permanent patients in such units. They were being returned just to reinforce their verbal warning. Gyatt had taken his mother away, and this was to confirm that Dadd Ward would not be in a position to have her back.

So where had he taken her? Another psychiatric unit? Where – and why – and why now? He forced his mind back over the mountain of time since Liz's abduction, Tracey Starmer's murder, the professional assassins dead, Liz at Gyatt's mercy. What had Joan Burnham said? Gerald Gyatt couldn't come to terms with his mother, couldn't deal with her. He closed his eyes, knowing he could push his mind no further. He slid the clothes back inside the brown paper and took out his mobile phone. It was answered on the third ring.

'Where are you?' Austin asked.

'I need to talk to you,' he said. 'Can you meet me?'

Austin encompassed surprise, irritation and concern in one silence, then repeated the question.

'In a layby, but I've been to Joan Burnham's house.' Then, unplanned, flooding to the surface came the fact that had disconcerted him the most. 'Austin?'

'Yes,' his friend answered, quietly responding to the appeal in his last word. 'What is it John?'

'This neighbour ...'

'Mrs Burnham?'

'What did you think of her?'

'I suppose ...' He took his time. 'I suppose I liked her. I warmed to her. She ...'

'You didn't see a resemblance to Liz?'

'I ... well, height, build, colouring when she was young. Her manner perhaps more – warmth, a feeling of natural generosity, yes,' he decided.

'Yes,' John confirmed, 'I found that more disturbing than what I learned about Gyatt – what he's done.'

At the end Austin asked, 'Why lumber himself with his mother now? What's your feeling?'

'He's tidying up – getting ready to leave, covering his tracks.'

'Be interesting to know what he told the psychiatrist. I'll get someone on to that.'

'Plus a search warrant for his house I would think,' John added.

'Not that straightforward,' Austin said and before John could muster his protests, he added, 'And it's complicated by the fact that Helen Moore has found a girl in an estate office in Boston with a tattooed wedding ring.'

CHAPTER 18

AUSTIN WAS GLAD to find that the street name he had been given meant the police car was discreetly parked two side streets away from the Boston estate agency.

Inspector Helen Moore, watching through her rearview mirror, leaned across and opened the passenger door for him as he walked up to the vehicle.

'We have a problem,' she said without preamble. 'This girl, Gwyneth Griffiths, is so defensive. As soon as I walked into the office her face turned to stone. Why, I'm not sure – as far as I know she's got nothing to hide but you never know, and I'm getting her checked out. It could just be she's naturally suspicious, or just doesn't like the police, or uniformed policewomen.'

'What have you told her?' he asked. 'And has any other officer been in?'

'Two bits of luck – for us anyway. Boston's overstretched, they've had a major pile-up on the A16. I took over some of this area to help speed the enquiries – and noticed the tattoo as she was working on her computer, before I'd even spoken.'

'And you said?' he asked.

'That we were having complaints about nuisance viewings, people asking to view large properties with no intention of buying. She didn't do much more than shake her head, and I left it at that, came out and called you.'

'Good, we can build on that. Last thing we want is her warning whoever has put his mark on her.'

Beside him Helen Moore shuddered. 'I saw a programme about the Nazis last night, the way they tattooed numbers on their Holocaust victims, then gassed them anyway. Sorry.'

He shook his head, refusing the need for apology. 'One tattooed girl, two men, we could be dealing with a multi-murderer.'

'No need for me to behave like a probationer.'

'Only worry when you stop being a little raw about man's inhumanity to his fellows,' he told her. 'So we'll build on your story, tell her as little as possible, learn as much as we can.'

Gwyneth Griffiths looked up, flicked her mass of waist-length brown hair back from her shoulders, and said nothing as Inspector Moore led the way into the estate agency.

'I'm Detective Inspector Austin,' he told her without preamble. 'I'd like to ask you a few questions....'

'I've already—' she began.

'Even so,' he said, 'if you don't mind. Unless of course your senior manager is here, or even the owner?' He looked down at her as she remained seated behind her counter, hands on her lap, for the moment out of sight.

'I am the manageress,' she said and looked at Helen Moore accusingly, 'as I've already told ...'

'And there is no one else here?' he asked, unperturbed.

She shook her head, then had to rearrange her hair again. What a nuisance all that must be, Austin thought, wondering about health and safety.

'No one else employed here?' he persisted.

'There's Mr Wood,' she snapped.

'And Mr Wood is?' he asked placidly.

'It's his business,' she said.

'And?'

'He comes some Saturdays, or if we have a really important client to show round a valuable property.' She tossed up her nose as she said this and looked at him almost insolently, as if she suspected he'd never been in anything bigger than a one-up, one-down. Austin sat down and pushed himself forward in the chair, so his eyes were on a level with hers.

'So, Mr Wood,' he began, 'you don't really see too much of him. He leaves you – trusts you, obviously – to deal with all the business enquiries.'

'Yes.' She arranged her hair so it hung free over the back of her chair. 'He does the outside work, I do the office.'

'And if you needed him urgently.'

'Oh, I wouldn't. We've got this business off to a tee.' It sounded like a quote, and there was confidence and self-satisfaction in this little Welsh girl now.

All hair and ego, Austin thought as he asked, 'But you could ring him if need be?'

'No, he rings me. He won't take calls – he says they just complicate life.'

I bet he does, and this just could be your Achilles' heel, my friend, Austin thought. This girl could not just ring to tell him what happened in the office day to day, she had to wait to be contacted. 'Is his life complicated?' he asked.

'He just likes to keep things simple.' Her voice rose to the top of its Welsh register, and she stood up abruptly, putting herself above his eyeline. 'He doesn't want to over-commit himself. I admire him for that too.'

'Admire.' Austin pondered the word as if to himself. In a mild conversational tone he asked, 'Why are you so defensive, Miss Griffiths? No one is accusing you, or Mr Wood, of anything. We are interested in people who may have been into your office, rather than your business arrangements.'

He saw the colour rise in her face, and she came back to sit down rather as if she needed to, and just as Inspector Moore's radio bleeped. Moore excused herself and went outside, moving out of sight to answer it.

'Looking round at your boards here,' Austin said, indicating the 'For Sale' pamphlets mounted on the wall boards, 'you seem to have quite a few large properties for sale. Is that unusual?'

'Mr Wood specializes in large properties.'

Again the pride in the voice, and the implication was 'my Mr Wood'. He knew the one thing he must not do was scare Mr Wood away. 'Nice to be involved in the quality end of the market then,' he said.

She nodded and smiled.

'So all I want to know is whether—' He pulled the pictures of the two men from his overcoat pocket '—these two have ever been into your agency.'

'Two inspectors coming asking questions?'

He had been branding her as completely gullible – but perhaps it was only Mr Wood who could delude his willing victim? He acknowledged her comment with a nod, as if making her a party to what they knew. 'As my colleague said we have had complaints, but now—' He paused to give her time to wonder about the pause '—it's more serious, we believe their objective is to target valuable fixtures.'

'Fixtures?' she queried, 'You mean like …'

'Old panelling, fireplaces, staircases, even old tiled or wooden floors. People who are converting old barns, churches, schools, chapels into houses, will pay fantastic sums for genuine features. It's a big operation. So it is in your boss's interest to know if these men are around.'

Gwyneth Griffiths looked down at the pictures Austin unrolled for her. She spread her hands to hold them flat, and for the first time he saw the tattooed ring clearly. His heart gave an extra thud of certainty. They were on the right scent, though he wished he had seen the hand of the murdered Tracey Starmer before it had been mutilated.

She put a finger on each man's face in turn. 'They looked different, their hair, and clothes, but yes. It was only last week.'

Her finger tapped each man with certainty. 'And they've already done what you said.' Her voice lilted upwards, but then she shook her head. 'Well, no, they didn't really. Mr Wood arranged to meet them at the property, but they never turned up. I expected them to come back to the office, but I've not seen them again.'

'Tell me exactly what happened,' he asked.

'They came in, enquiring about a property we have on the coast, a real big farm, with holiday let cottages, its own beach ...'

'For a small office you really do deal in big properties.'

'It's Mr Wood,' she said, tossing back the hair, 'he has contacts in London.'

'Oh! I see,' he said mildly, squashing all ironic thoughts. 'Go on with what you were saying ... its own beach ...'

'Yes. Mr Wood says it's a property the National Trust really ought to be interested in buying. When these two men came in I couldn't wait for him to ring so I could tell him we had possible customers. And he was just as excited, wanted to know all about them, particularly what they looked like, everything. Well, as I told him, they said they were looking for investment property, something with holiday lets that would bring in a good annual return on their money. I thought we had a real chance of a sale.'

'So Mr Wood came here to meet them and take them to the property.'

'No – it was done by phone. He gave me a time for them to meet him at the property, but he rang back to say they never turned up. He waited and waited,' she said, then added with a dismissive shrug, 'but I think it was out of their league anyway.'

And she, he thought, is in the web of a much bigger spider than she realizes. If it was her boss who had put his cynical indelible mark on her finger, then it was highly likely Wood was also Gyatt QC. Wood the absentee boss was also Gyatt the absentee QC – but he dare not produce Gyatt's photo, dare not risk her warning him the moment he next contacted her. His dilemma was confounded by the knowledge that his duty was also one of care for this young woman.

Inspector Moore came back into the property shop and, watching the girl's face, Austin saw exactly what Helen meant about her face turning to stone. Inspector Moore looked back at her with much the same lack of expression. 'The two men,' she said, nodding down to the photos. 'They've been dealt with, so no need to worry Miss Grainger further.'

Grainger? Austin looked from the inspector to the girl, and now watched the transformation from house to alley cat as the girl took in the name said so meaningfully. If cats snarl, Miss Grainger showed how, her hair hanging unnoticed over her eyes.

'So you'll lose me this job, just like your precious oppo did in Wisbeach! She let me down just when I'd started in an estate agency there. Now you ...'

'I see no need for us to go any further in this matter,' Austin interrupted, 'if—'

'Miss Geraldine Grainger is keeping her nose clean,' Inspector Moore put in. 'Nine months down, fifteen to go, I believe.'

Austin assimilated the situation; Helen Moore was showing him the way to ensure that Gwyneth, or Geraldine, did not think of warning off her employer.

'The straight and narrow's not easy,' he said. 'As far as we're concerned there's no reason for Mr Wood to know we've even been here. The men ... have been dealt with, so ... he's no further worry on that score.'

She pushed back her hair, and Austin saw she had calmed down enough to recognize a let-out when she saw it. 'I shan't tell him, you can be sure of that.' Her hands came together, and her fingers rested over the tattooed promise.

Back in the car, Austin said, 'That gives us breathing space, but in the meantime I'd like Miss Property Shop kept under surveillance. What I'd really like to do is take her into protective custody.' He paused and shrugged his shoulders. 'That's obviously not an option. But I wouldn't like her to come to the same end as Tracey Starmer.'

'So this appointment to view?' she queried. 'Is it possible this is how Gyatt/Wood managed to track down our, or rather, his assassins?'

'She did say he particularly asked what these potential customers looked like,' Austin considered. 'He'd have had to be able to see them without being seen himself, then follow them a fair old way from Boston back to Stetford Mill.'

'They wouldn't expect to be followed, and from the receipts we found in the car at the Mill they liked their pub lunches. My guess is they'd stop for a meal, so it might not have been too difficult to keep track of them.'

'Hmm … a day or two to make his plans, then in and bang, bang, bang, both men dead. It's possible, but if we assume all that, what has he done with Liz Makepeace? Has he still got her?'

'We have to assume he has. Until we find proof to the contrary,' she said, 'and the longer the search goes on the more likely it is that he's keeping her alive, a prisoner for his own ends, a bargaining tool perhaps?'

'But there's a terrible complication.' He told her of Gyatt fetching his mother away from Dadd Ward, the private asylum she had been in for years.

Startled by this revelation she sat assessing the implications, and there was consternation in her voice as she asked, 'So has he got two women locked away somewhere?'

'And are they together?' Even as he proposed this he shook his head. 'Doesn't feel likely somehow.'

'No,' she agreed, 'and if he's killed three times … far more likely he has disposed of one or the other.'

'Or both,' Austin said, and was then shocked by his reaction. 'You've heard Liz and John Cannon's history?'

'Yes, Don Lovett made a point of telling me.'

Don Lovett! Austin had a sudden image of his near-monosyllabic chief inspector behind his desk, scowling into his phone, talking love.

'And we shouldn't forget some kidnap victims are hidden for years, and then released,' she added.

If it was meant to help, it didn't. 'Liz Makepeace used to be afraid of nothing,' he said, remembering the woman always ready for undercover work, always ready to play a part, take on a dangerous, devious role to bring law breakers to justice. 'But it's time we found her.'

CHAPTER 19

J OHN COULD NOT accuse Austin of keeping him ill informed. The confirmation of the tattooed ring was followed by the news that an underwater search team had found parts of the Porsche chassis in a lake to the rear of Coupledyke House. The mangled parts were on their way to forensics.

Austin had finished this call with, 'The Trap's about halfway between Streetly and Boston. I'll see you there.'

John drove towards home unable to throw off the feeling of essential things left undone. Was there a vital question he had not asked? Should he have driven straight to that private asylum? He knew the mere mention of Inspector Austin's name would not have given him immediate access there, as it had with Joan Burnham. But he still felt he was doing the one thing he should not do – and that was drive away, go home. It felt like giving up.

When he neared his pub he thought Paul had opened it, against his specific instructions. There were several vehicles in his car park. He slowed to count – five, plus Paul's – before swinging in through the arch to the old stables. He walked out towards the main entrance, but it was locked.

The back door was open. He paused inside the porch listening to the sound of quite a few voices coming from behind the closed kitchen door. Then he felt overwhelmed by the sight of Liz's walking boots and wellingtons side by side in the corner. He swayed back, leaned on the wall, closed his eyes, startled the next moment to find a hand encompassing his elbow.

'Thought I heard a car,' Paul said. 'Come through to the bar. We're in here.'

He allowed himself to be led and was surprised to find a fire lit, Hoskins in his normal seat and an easel set up in front of him, with the beginnings of a portrait of the old poacher on the canvas.

Hoskins rose and gestured John to a seat near the fire. 'Come on, boy,' he said, making for the business side of the bar. 'I'll get you a brandy.'

'Good of you,' John said, for a second slipping into his old ironic relationship with his most regular customer. 'But what's happening here? Who's here?'

'Conference in the kitchen. Austin, Helen Moore, DS Maddern and someone higher up ...' He paused as the door opened and Austin came in. Behind him they glimpsed a tall man with a heavily braided cap leading a purposeful exodus.

Austin closed the door, nodded at John, then walked over to the easel and stood silent, looking at the newly begun painting.

'So it's hush-hush, is it?' the sitter asked. 'Or are you going to tell us what's going on?'

'It is hush-hush,' Austin confirmed, pulling a chair next to Hoskins. Paul too pulled in a chair, so the four of them sat in a near circle. 'But I'm going to tell you quite a lot, because I need your co-operation.'

'You want me to stay 'ere,' Hoskins guessed.

'I do,' he answered, 'holding the fort.'

Given a role, the old man straightened in his seat.

'The wider picture,' Austin went on, 'coming from the Met is that the godfather of the newly organized group is waiting on the death of the man they know as the Dry Cleaner. He's been waiting a time now, and he is not a patient man. He's old-school Mafia, but his troops are murmuring too at the waste of time, but so far murmur is all they dare do.'

'But he's killed these hitmen, hasn't he? This Dry Cleaner, this Gyatt chap?' Hoskins frowned, hands gripping his knees as if to hold tight to the facts, wanting to understand.

'Yes,' Austin agreed, 'but we have undercover men who can, who are going to, pass on a message that the opposite has happened, that the contract on Gyatt has been carried out.'

'So the deaths at the mill will be covered up,' Paul said.

'And as soon as the gang think the Dry Cleaner is out of the way they'll begin operations,' John added.

Austin nodded. 'Then the Met swoops on a dozen addresses they've been watching for months, and the guys in Paris do the same.'

'Meanwhile Gyatt, who is not dead?' John hung the question in the air.

'I'm trusting we can devise a plan to trap the man through this lead in Boston.'

'And meantime, Liz?' John questioned, then added, 'And Gyatt's mother, of course.'

'Helen Moore is to restart investigations from the private asylum. Some preliminary work's been done, and we believe Gyatt is now driving a black Vauxhall Zafira. All the leads are being followed, local interviews, sightings, as well as all the searches we set up after Stetford Mill. Every stone we can think of is being turned.' He pressed this last urgently on Cannon.

He acknowledged it with a brief nod. 'But you can't issue a warrant for the arrest of a man who's supposed to have been murdered. So what's the idea?'

'The property shop manageress, Miss Gwyneth Griffiths, the name she's currently using ...' Austin filled them in on all that was known of her and the way the estate agency was run, ending that according to this girl the details of the substantial properties all came from London.

'From where the assassins were following the same leads,' John said.

'Somewhere there must be a London office,' Austin went on. 'The source of the details and keys Tracey Starmer drove here.'

'All beginning to build a picture,' Paul said.

'They have one outstanding property on their books at the moment – an extensive farmhouse, with land, private beach and holiday let cottages,' Austin told them. 'If we could send a convincing enough customer to Boston there's just the chance ...'

'He'll snap up the bait,' Hoskins concluded.

'It's something we have to try while we wait on ...' Austin paused. Having nearly said 'the big end of this operation', he quickly substituted 'the London boys'.

Paul had been listening intently. 'You know this sounds just like the property I've been looking for all my life. Just right to open my residential art school,' he said.

Austin grinned.

'You bugger!' Paul exclaimed, 'You were planning something like that!'

'Hoping, old boy, hoping,' Austin said, 'but seriously you would do this? There are plain-clothes men I could use ...'

'But I'll be more convincing,' he said, 'the real thing, and high time I was allowed to put my nose outside these doors.'

Too late to ring the estate office that evening, every preparation was made ready for the next day. Austin made arrangements for Paul to have bank referees should he need to prove his viability as a potential buyer. There would also be a Mercedes on hand for him to drive to the estate agency.

The next morning, a couple of minutes after nine they were all four reassembled. A Mercedes was drawn up outside The Trap. Paul had on a sharkskin grey suit with a black polo neck shirt, and John, who had elected to go with him, a black pinstriped suit, the last one he had bought in London, with an open-necked white and black striped shirt.

'Bloody toffs,' Hoskins approved.

Paul punched in the estate office number and all four waited. As the call was answered he turned his back on the group and assumed the proprietary air of a man with serious wealth anxious to make an investment.

The conversation that followed was fairly predictable until Paul took on an irritated manner and said, 'Well, that's hardly very satisfactory. I would have liked to view right away, today if possible. I have an interest in another similar property in Cornwall. I don't want to risk losing out on one property just because I have to wait to view yours. Surely ...'

There was the sound of a raised placatory voice at the other end of the phone.

'Well, perhaps I'll come and fetch some details. Very well,' he said and folded the mobile.

'Butter in my hands,' he told them. 'We can pick up the details, and she'll arrange a viewing ASAP.'

'Which won't be until her Mr Wood decides to ring her,' Austin said.

This was to be far sooner than any of them anticipated, though Paul and John both realized all was not well as soon as they walked into the estate office. The girl did not look at all at ease, certainly far from delighted to see possible customers for the biggest property on their books.

'Good morning, gentlemen.' She was nervous and John was instantly alert. 'You've come about the Bartlett estate?'

'We spoke on the phone,' Paul confirmed, staring fixedly at the abundant pre-Raphaelite hair, 'and if we set up our art college locally you must come and be a model for my students.'

He could not have said anything better to bring the girl on to their side. She blushed, stood straighter and swept back the mane. 'I have the details ready for you.' She lifted a folder from the desk and handed it to him. Then she paused and frowned. 'Unfortunately, Mr Wood ...'

'Mr Wood?' Paul repeated.

'My employer, the owner. Well, he telephoned this morning ...'

'Good! That's just what we wanted, wasn't it? So now ...'

'Unfortunately,' she began again.

'Unfortunately?'

John watched her intently and saw genuine discomfort.

'Yes, unfortunately Mr Wood is unable to let anyone view for another few days. I think he said there's some problem with the vendors.'

'A few days?' Paul expostulated. 'Doesn't the man want to sell the property? Why advertise it?'

'What did he actually say?' John asked quietly.

She looked at him sharply and for a moment he wondered if this worldly-wise young woman saw through their pretence, but as Paul, with immaculate timing, threw down the folder she had given him and began to turn away, she added, 'What he actually said was he needed just a few more days to tidy things up, then he ...' She paused, her jaw sliding sideways across her teeth as she considered whether she should go on.

Paul turned back, glanced from the girl back to the folder. 'Then he...?'

'Then he'll be ready for a quick deal on this one.'

'Really.' Paul almost made the word a sentence, then he ran his gaze over the girl in a way that made his 'that sounds more interesting' very personal indeed.

'You should get an Oscar,' John said as they walked away from the shop.

'Villain trained in college dramatic society.' He tucked the folder under his arm. 'So where to now? As if I need to ask.'

'The Bartlett Farm estate,' John confirmed and once in the car opened the folder and found a map complete with road numbers.

'Shouldn't take us more than half an hour,' Paul said. 'So does this all suggest Mr Wood is planning to make a run for it? Is he collecting his assets and his mother, ready to make for a foreign hideaway?'

'If he's tidying things up after being told he has a possible customer,' John said, his mind on more immediate possibilities, 'he could be there now.'

'What do you think that means, tidying up?' Paul asked.

'What do you?'

'You found empty boxes at Creighton Hall, and then money stuffed into sacks at Stetford Mill – is that right?'

'Right.'

'So it could be something like that he has to tidy up,' Paul suggested, 'and don't you have the feeling that he's finally being driven into a corner?'

'I know he's handy with a gun,' John replied and took Liz's revolver from his pocket.

'I hope that's not for me!' Paul exclaimed, the car veering to the wrong side of the road.

'Your option,' John told him. 'I've got mine.'

'No thanks, then.'

'Perhaps as well,' he said. 'Gyatt's obviously an expert. There won't be time for further play-acting when we do confront him.'

The implication, and the focussed determination in Cannon's voice, kept Paul silent as they neared the stretch of coast where the Bartlett estate must be. They found the property north of the fun and water parks of Skegness and Ingoldmells, beyond the scope of pinewood picnic sites.

Confronted by locked gates, many 'Private' signs – and the knowledge that Gyatt could have come straight here when he heard there was a possible customer – they took a lane running along the southern boundary. Even this was stoutly fenced with barbed wire coiled along the top.

'We should have come in combat gear,' Paul said.

'The property has its own beach,' John reminded him. 'It should be easier to get in that way.'

They parked and walked to marram-grass-topped dunes, to look down over a splendid beach, golden and deserted in bright morning sun. They could see neither fences nor buildings as they moved beyond the dunes, but once out of the shelter of the sand-hills the wind from the north-east was arctic. They struggled to make headway; the sand, dry as dust, came over their shoe tops with every step and the wind whipped stinging gusts of sand up into their faces. Cannon indicated they should move nearer to the sea's edge where the tide was on the turn and had ebbed enough to leave a narrow stretch of firmer going.

'Look good on a photo,' Paul shouted. 'You'd never guess how cold it was.'

John laid a hand on his arm and pointed inland.

CHAPTER 20

A N EXTENSIVE BRICK farmhouse lay in the centre of two barn
and stable complexes. Viewing it in any other circumstances
John would have said it had a pleasant, open aspect, a
welcoming appearance – from the sea. A contrast to the barbed
wire and the 'Keep Out' notices surrounding its land sides.

'Phone Austin, tell him where we are,' Paul said, gripping the
end of the boundary fence where it stopped at the beach.

'You phone him.' Cannon tossed him the phone. 'Punch one.
Then catch me up.' He indicated the way he intended to go, alongside the fence, then in towards the first block of barn conversions.
He couldn't risk an argument with Austin, and he didn't wait for
an answer from Paul, just made his way through scattered pines
and rhododendron bushes.

The new windows in the first barns faced the sea, but the doors
were at the side and back. Every sense alert, he approached the
side door. He shook his head at the single Yale-type lock, took a
credit card from his wallet and slipping the flexy plastic between
door jamb and lock had the door open as quick as if he had a key.

He stepped inside and listened. He was surprised just how
warm it did feel out of the wind. Taking the revolver from his
pocket he went rapidly and silently from room to room, and
remembering the likelihood of large quantities of money being on
the premises – and other things he had found secreted away
during his career – he swiftly inspected every cupboard.

This block of properties had obviously never been used; everywhere was too pristine, as if the decorators had just left. But he persisted with his search, impelled by a mounting feeling of urgency. A sound behind him made him swing round, crouching, gun in both hands.

Paul grimaced, held up the phone as if expecting the messenger to be blamed for the message. 'Whatever,' Cannon mouthed, and held out a hand for the mobile, then moved ahead up the stairs.

They went through each of the buildings on the south side of the farmhouse, each door yielding as easily as the first, with Paul carefully and quietly closing them as they left.

So they came back to the farmhouse proper. He reasoned that if *he* had something, or someone, to hide he would choose this old farmhouse. The front, sea-facing façade had a modest pillared portico cloaking a robust front door, which would have heavy mortise locks and bolts, and on this side all the old windows had external shutters. It was clear that whatever modernization and conversions the outbuildings had undergone, this was all original. The idea to tap into the holiday industry had perhaps not come early enough and funds had run out, or perhaps some other tragedy had overtaken the owners.

'We'll go in from the back, through the old farmyard,' he said. Both turned then stopped in the same second, each catching the same hot, acrid smell in the air. Petrol, diesel? Fumes of some kind.

'An engine,' Paul said.

'A tractor, perhaps.' Cannon reviewed the lie of the land, the 'Trespassers Will Be Prosecuted' signs, the locked gates, the distance from the main road – and shook his head. 'Somebody's here,' he decided.

'Gyatt,' Paul whispered and Cannon nodded, while wondering if the clearing up the man had to do needed a tractor. A digger?

They found that the farmhouse was built like a blind 'E'; outhouses formed the end arms, and had no doubt housed fuel, probably including an old washhouse or back kitchen.

Cannon intended to inspect the nearest outhouses, then go systematically through the farm, and after that the outhouses opposite, but some sixth sense, some lingering animal instinct in the human psyche had kicked in. His breathing quickened, his nerve ends felt so super-charged they hurt – and as if to reinforce his instincts the wind gusted that choking gassy smell to them again.

He was about to move into the first outhouse when Paul gripped his arm and nodded towards the farmhouse. Paul's eye had been caught by a tapering wedge of black between door and frame 'That door's open,' he said.

'House first then.' Cannon breathed and led the way quickly and silently to the door. He pushed it opened, stopping the moment it made contact with the stone floor, the gap wide enough for them to sidle in. The door led straight into the kitchen. Inside, the warmth struck him even more than it had in the barns

The kitchen was slabbed, a solid fuel cooker at the far side, a wooden draining board to a stone sink, nothing else. He took the left room first, empty and nothing leading from that. From the right of the kitchen they emerged from under the stairs into the hall. The murky fanlight above the front door revealed a black and white tiled hall. Rooms to right and left he had calculated from the shuttered windows would be sitting room and dining room, each room of exactly the same proportions. Before he could stop him Paul had taken the left-hand room, so he took the right. There were built-in cupboards to one side – these were empty, and he met Paul back at the bottom of the stairs.

He led the way. They again took left and right rooms at the front. These behind the shuttered windows were dim, close and empty. Moving to the back of the house, it still felt warm, though the sun did not touch these bedrooms, and the windows overlooking the farmyard were bare. He was turning to the left when he heard Paul gasp, and turned to see him pointing into the right-hand room.

He moved to Paul's side. Then his breathing stopped, his life put on hold. He had seen the photographs of the Stetford Mill scenario, and here was a repeat. Here was the same inflatable bed against the wall, the same covering – a humped and rumpled sleeping bag.

In the eternity of seconds it took him to make his legs move again he heard Paul swearing, though it sounded more like a prayer. He stumbled over to stand above the piled sleeping bag and prayed that whoever it was, it would not be Liz. With a sound like an indrawn gasp of pain, he stooped, touched, lifted the cover, a little, then higher, then threw it aside. Nothing.

'God Almighty,' Paul breathed, 'how much more ...' He did not finish the sentence as John stooped to place a hand on the mattress.

'Cold,' he said. No one alive had lain there recently.

Paul had watched, horrified, but now backed out of room shaking his head. On the landing he put out a hand as if to steady himself and made contact with the enormous old radiator below the window – and leapt away as if stung or shocked. He stumbled and fell to his knees.

'What? What!'

'That's hot!' he exclaimed, then quietly repeated, 'That bloody thing's hot.'

John scowled, doubting, then went forward and clamped a hand on the great metal ribs, released them just as quickly and stood staring out of the window into the yard. 'These places don't have nice Potterton boilers. They have ...'

'Separate boiler houses, in my experience,' Paul said, 'and for an old place this size probably a furnace....'

'Coke fumes,' Cannon said, 'that's what we smelt out there. Someone stoking a furnace.'

'Not to heat an empty house.'

The both instinctively looked out of the landing window down on to the yard, and both drew in astonished breaths. A man came from the far side of the yard carrying a large, soft kind of brief-case, a size useful for many things.

'That's the man Hoskins described,' Paul said, voice low as if there was some chance of being overheard. 'The man I sketched.'

'Gyatt,' John confirmed and taking Paul's arm made to draw him back from the window, but in the same second the man looked up. That he saw them Cannon had no doubt, for though his stride did not seem to falter, he spun on his heels, mirror image of many a QC he'd seen spin round a High Court room to confront or confound a witness – or impress the jury. His pose spoke of a man in control, of doing just what he intended – and it infuriated Cannon.

He raised the revolver, knocked out a pane of glass with the butt, then aimed and shot. The window frame impeded his aim and he missed. Gyatt ran, a powerfully built man, but with no airs, no control now, he was just a scared man, a criminal, scarpering.

Cannon thrust his phone back to Paul again. 'Austin,' he said, 'tell him.' Then he leapt down the stairs, out, across the yard, the coke fumes stronger as he sprinted the way Gyatt had gone, round towards the far side and the barns they had not inspected.

On this side the rhododendrons grew in greater profusion, the pines more closely packed, and he could see neither Gyatt nor the vehicle he must have arrived in. He paused to listen. The sea wind, redolent with pine, whined its passage through conifers and ever-green, but Cannon could see no regular path or trackway. Then came a snap, a broken twig or branch, the sound of something or someone falling some way to his left – inland. He pushed into the shrubbery, redoubled the effort as he heard a vehicle start, then the high protest of an engine and the screech of tyres as a car was recklessly reversed, turned, then driven away.

Seconds later he emerged on to a lane much like the one they had taken on the far side of this property, but seconds too late, and while it could have been a black Ford Zafira driving away at speed, he was not certain.

He felt sick with his failure. So near ... But he must get back, the car must be reported and rest of the property searched. He turned but the shrubbery had swung back into place and he could not see where he had just pushed his way through. Then a few metres away a bough hung, half broken, its white pith fresh. This was where Gyatt had pushed his way out. He turned back into the bushes at this point, parting them with his arms, and he had not gone more than twenty paces when he saw the black bag, snagged and lodged in a gnarled old rhododendron. His heart leapt as he reviewed the image of Gyatt in the yard a few minutes ago. The man had certainly not been wearing gloves, but in any case his reason told him there must be enough DNA in that bag to ... 'Got you, Gyatt!' he said between gritted teeth.

With care, and his handkerchief, he began to untangle the bag from the ancient bush. Hardly had he moved one branch than the bag plummeted to the ground and landed with a solid thud. There was certainly more than just estate agent's pamphlets in there. Even so, when he did manage to lift it clear, he was astonished just how heavy it was. Had it been something like a plumber's bag, with wrenches, spanners and whatever, it could not have been heavier.

He curbed any wish to look inside until after he rejoined Paul. It comforted him to know that even if the police never found the car, he would have far more damning forensic evidence on and in this bag.

By the time he had run back he was surprised Gyatt had managed to carry the bag with such seeming nonchalance. But all thoughts of Gyatt were wiped from his mind as he came to where Paul stood in the centre of the yard, without a vestige of colour in his face. He turned stricken eyes on Cannon as he came nearer, pointed like the proverbial figure of doom to where the doors of two of the outhouses stood open.

Still carrying the bag, Cannon walked over to the first open door – a coke store, with a shovelling hatch through to what must be the furnace house. He glanced back at Paul, but he had remained where he was. He went on to the next open door, and there was the furnace. A great monster that half filled the place, solid, rusted, but around its door, about the size of that to a normal oven, glowed red and fearsome evidence of the fire within.

He looked back at Paul once more, who shook his head and looked down. There must still be more for him to see, still something he had not discovered. Stepping over the threshold of the furnace room, he felt the heat more intensely – and then the nausea.

To one side was a stout wooden table, the kind a carpenter or a butcher would need to do his work – and on the table was a shrouded shape. There was no deceptive thickness to this cover. This white shroud was thin cotton and revealed the shape of a woman.

He realized that Paul had not touched the body; the shock of discovery had driven him out into the yard. He had not lifted the sheet to see the face. With some final attempt at a wordless deal with the Almighty, Cannon did what Paul had not been able to.

It was not Liz. Cannon sank to his knees because suddenly his legs had no strength to hold him, the forgotten weight of the bag in his hand thudding down by his side. He released it with horror – now he knew what it contained, now he knew why it was so heavy – and he had carried it to its intended destination.

He clung to the edge of the table through the draped sheet, successful mendicant, the sacrifice not his.

'John?'

He had forgotten Paul. He turned to see him in the doorway. 'It's not Liz,' he said.

Paul gave a strangled kind of cry and came to kneel by him. 'I should have looked, I'm sorry, so sorry, I just … it was the …' he paused and raised a hand to indicate what was above them, then took John's arm and they helped each other to their feet. 'Just the laying out, the sheet, it's so … graphic.'

'Sick,' John said, anger now giving him back his strength, 'but we've got him. I've got his bag of tools with as much DNA as any forensic department could ever hope for.'

'Tools?' Paul queried, then glancing from table to furnace, he muttered, 'Oh my God! But who is she, if …'

'We must look again.' John was calm now, able to deal, able to come to conclusions. He took the extreme edge of the sheet and folded it meticulously back. What struck him first was the extreme whiteness of the woman's face. Once the blood stops pumping the complexion soon drains of its colour, but this woman was more like a fragile plant that had been deprived of light for many years, growing ever more white and wan.

'I think it could be his mother,' John said. 'She has the look of one who's been incarcerated.'

Paul came closer. 'I think you're right. Gyatt has that same angular nose.'

CHAPTER 21

USTIN AND HELEN Moore had just finished following up the forensic evidence on the Porsche engine number, and had confirmed it as the vehicle owned by Gyatt, when Cannon spoke to him. 'Stay where you are, I'll be there,' he told him.

Before Austin reached his car he had marshalled every man they could muster to throw a cordon around the whole area. He issued Gyatt's description, and the possible car he was driving. They were all to make this operation top priority: 'use stingers, anything to stop him.'

He sat in his car and rang the Yard, asking for Don Lovett. The request was met by a pregnant pause, a click, and then a voice that was not Lovett, and certainly not one he wished to hear. He had been put through to the press bureau, which as far as Austin was concerned was for police officers with little common sense and no discretion. He felt mildly insulted.

'I do understand the situation,' he said, keeping his voice low, level and infinitely polite. 'I have a new situation, plus another murder at my end, and I wanted to make Lovett aware …'

'This is about matters above the importance of individuals,' he was told.

'God help us all,' he said and rung off – unwisely rung off, he knew that. There would be many other occasions he would have to deal with the director of public affairs and he would probably now be noted down as difficult, or having attitude.

His phone rang again. This time it was the assistant commissioner, whose jurisdictions included the press bureau. Austin's difficult attitude had, it seemed, already been snitched on. This conversation was also brief, but this time not terminated by Austin. The assistant commissioner reminded Austin that the situation was, as he understood it, exactly as Austin wanted. 'You're dealing with the abduction and so forth.'

'That's correct, sir,' Austin had answered, 'but ...'

There had been some kind of a rumble about 'so what was the problem', and the call ended.

He started his car, aware that his attempt to reach Lovett had made him sure of several things: the news of the supposed success of the hitmen in taking out the Dry Cleaner had reached the right ears, the new organization had swung into action, and the London end of the police operation must be just about to, or just have, gone live. In many centres, not just in London, officers could even at this moment be breaking their way into upmarket homes, sordid council flats, offices, warehouse, prostitutes' haunts ... the list was endless. Austin knew it all, had seen the fear in the eyes of the guilty, the resentment of the nearly innocent, and the shuttered faces of his own men doing unpleasant things to uphold and restore law.

He drove, reflecting there had been other swoops like this, and bigger – and would be again – but the Met's press bureau was going to have a very different story to handle when Gyatt was finally, publicly named. A QC who had killed four times – four times to date – before they had caught up with him. He could see the news headlines: 'Did his position protect him?'; 'QC allowed to go on murdering!'

He was on the main coast road driving north towards the area of the Bartlett Estate, and was cognisant of unmarked police cars in laybys, glimpsing the red stripes of patrolling cars as he drove. But no reports had come through, no sightings. Once the first half hour, then the first hour, had gone, the chances of netting Gyatt escaping from the scene were probably gone.

He came to a halt believing he had followed Paul's description of where they had parked the Mercedes to the letter, but this lane was empty – though where the tide had ebbed he found and followed two sets of men's footprints.

Except for the wind, it seemed abnormally quiet. CIS would be on their way, but he had undoubtedly reached the scene first. He braced himself for the task of trying to give John some positive information, some hope.

He could say it would soon be possible to issue a warrant for Gyatt – but would that help Liz Makepeace? It could expedite an outcome no one wanted, particularly as Gyatt had seemingly already disposed of his mother. He anticipated finding Cannon fairly distraught, a man fretting for action. But what more could they do? Searches, observation, all he could think of was already in place. His experience told him the best option was to go back to the evidence, retread the ground, perhaps have another session with the chart on the dartboard.

He came to a momentary stop where the tide had left quite a pile – many hundreds – of razorshells, young, delicate, long shells far from maturity, and wondered what calamity had caused their demise. He stepped delicately around the mound, remembering how he had many times watched and wondered at his father shaving with a cut-throat razor, fascinated by the audible swish with which the blade was deftly angled around cheeks, chin and throat, dealing swiftly with soap and stubble. His father still persisted in the old practice, and these days often nicked himself. Austin was very afraid there was going to be the equivalent of bleeding when the warrant was issued for Gyatt. He did not see how his father's old Chambers could escape unscathed; in fact, they would be besieged by the media once the word was out.

There was something he could do once he had dealt with this latest murder. He would ring his father and without giving any information at all get him to invite Mr Parmar down to Dorset for a holiday. Take no refusal, he would say.

He saw Paul immediately he was level with the main farm building, and began to walk inland. He couldn't not see him, for the artist was sitting on the front step, staring down between his feet and obviously unaware of Austin's arrival. He was quite close before he was heard. Paul started, shot to his feet, then clapped a hand to his chest.

'Have you seen John?' he demanded.

'No, should I?'

'He finished searching the whole property, and left, gone back, he said, retracing steps. He said you'd understand.'

'Are you all right?' he asked, for Paul looked in need of some immediate care. He was obviously in shock, and as Austin took his arm he could feel him shaking. 'Come on, old chap, let's get out of this wind.'

Paul started with him, then stopped. 'I'm sorry,' he said, 'I can't ... I ...' He broke from Austin's grasp and fell back against one of the pillars covering his face with his hands, and began to sob in great, shuddering, uncontrollable spasms.

'Bodies are not—'

'No! No!' The denial was violent. 'Not the body – shrouded – I didn't look. I didn't look! I should've ... Cannon looked. He'd thought it was ... then when he looked and it wasn't ... his knees just let him down.'

Austin put an arm around his shoulders and tried to urge him around the corner, to shelter him, but Paul pulled away and gazed towards the sea as if he needed all its rolling power to cleanse his mind.

'You'll wait here?'

Paul nodded and Austin felt he had little option but to let him go, while wondering where the hell Cannon had gone. Where had he taken the hired Mercedes?

It was when Austin saw the shrouded body and thought of the visual impact on a man who earned his living from depicting scenes and images that he realized why Paul was so shaken. The draped sheet over the woman's body could have been a marble depiction of some excessive Victorian statement of grief. The sight of a man, a friend, fallen to his knees must have made it a classic memorial to mourning.

No one had mentioned the black bag that stood next to the sheeted body and table. He pulled a pair of latex gloves from his pocket. He stooped to look at the bag. Then aware of the over-whelming heat of the place he gagged as he also caught that putrid meat smell. One hand clamped over his mouth, he touched the catch of the bag. It fell open immediately, to reveal a small, solid saw, the type a butcher uses for bones, and several large knives.

No classical images, no echo of cold stone memorials here. He clamped nose and mouth to control the rising bile and lifted the sheet to view the woman's face: suffocation, he thought, regis-tering the bluish tinge around the mouth, the seeming tension of the neck as if she had fought and striven for every last breath. He felt a terrible pity for the woman, not only incarcerated for years, now murdered – and if Cannon and Jefferson had not intervened, then to be butchered and cremated in pieces by her son.

He held his breath long enough to look down at the face, hard, bitter, even in death, and remember what her neighbour had said: 'she was certifiable when Gerald was a little boy.' He reflected that if only her husband had been a stronger man and arranged for psychiatric treatment when first needed, there might have been a decent family instead of one suicide, one murder and one murderer.

Thankfully he strode out of the hellish charnel house with its added acrid smell of that ancient coke furnace. He was relieved to see that Paul had come to stand, leaning against the opposite outhouses. He was also relieved to hear the sound of vehicles coming up the main drive. They must have used bolt and wire cutters to open the gates.

'Paul, I can get you a lift straight back to your own place, rather than The Trap,' he suggested, 'for a break.'

Paul pulled a face, then straightened up. 'No, I've done my prima donna bit, I'll go back, see it out now.' They began to walk to meet the oncoming police cars. 'I've no idea where John's gone, you know. He just asked me if I minded waiting for you, then took off.'

It was the middle of the afternoon before they arrived back at The Trap, to see the Mercedes in the car park. 'Thank God,' Austin muttered.

But they were met by Hoskins at the back door. He looked ruffled, as if he had run his hand continually through his grey hair from back to front. 'About time somebody came,' he greeted them.

'Where's John?' Paul asked.

'Gone. Just in and out he was.'

'Did he say where he was going?'

Hoskins shook his head; gave an unamused laugh. 'He wasn't in the mood to answer questions. Some traveller from a brewery caught him while he was swapping cars. When the man got out his order book, I thought he was going to hit him.'

Austin's phone rang; he saw it was the Yard. He walked back outside to take it. It was Lovett. 'Upset the press bureau then,' Don Lovett stated, but there was an upbeat note to his voice.

'It's gone well?' Austin asked.

'Bloody has,' Lovett rejoiced.

'Well, we've waited long enough.'

'You've got any other body?'

Austin told him.

'Unless you hear from me, you can issue your warrant for Gyatt midday tomorrow. But no news of the hostage?' Pausing to hear there was not, he added, 'Poor bugger.'

'Will you arrange a search of Gyatt's London flat?' Austin asked.

'I'll lead it myself. What about his Chambers?' Then he paused as if waiting for confirmation of something he knew.

'My father's old Chambers,' Austin said.

'I'd heard that.'

'I asked his clerk, who is still there, to let me know if Gyatt put in an appearance.'

'Leave that to you then,' Lovett said. 'I'll let you know what we find at his flat.'

Austin felt comforted by his support for his own unfinished end of the case, and oddly deflated by the upbeat tones of a man who had successfully brought off his part of the operation.

He moved further away from the building, out towards where John had parked the Mercedes, and rang his father.

CHAPTER 22

CANNON HAD NOT burdened Hoskins with either what he intended or the fact that it was the old man himself who was inspiring the course of action.

And what he was doing was quite illogical according to all his training – or even his common sense – but he had moved beyond reasoning. His momentum was now powered by instinct. An instinct he was listening to because he could not escape it, but its conception had been of Alan Hoskins' making.

Cannon had, often reluctantly, listened over his bar counter to debates such as how you knew someone was looking at you, even when that person could be behind a window some distance off. Hoskins' ideas could encompass the whole bar, and one night the old poacher had related how, very early one morning, he had been walking past an isolated cottage, and the word fire had come into his mind. He said he had stopped, had a good look round, but seen and smelt nothing. Later he learned that a bedroom in the cottage had been completely burnt out. 'Now 'ow did I know that!' He had tapped the side of his nose. 'Never doubt yourself.' No one had taken him up on that one.

So this was the reason, the slim chance, the instinct he was following as he drove back to Streetly West, to Gyatt's home address, and to the neighbour who had reminded him of Liz – and there, as he was sure Austin would have quoted, 'was the rub'. At the pit bottom of his mind he wondered if he was going back because Joan Burnham had reminded him so much of Liz – or was it just his yearning for her, or even just someone like her?

He did not risk passing where he knew the surveillance van was. He parked in a shopping centre car park that was beginning to empty at this tail-end of the afternoon. He explored the area, looking for the back way into the Victorian houses. There would certainly have been tradesmen's entrances, side roads for deliveries.

He was walking the third side of the square of properties that included Gyatt's house when he came to a gap, a narrow no-man's land between the back gardens. No more than the first metre of the path was regularly trodden, probably by children popping in to hide. Beyond that odd bushes, plus ash and birch saplings, had sprung up and flourished. Anyone easily deterred would have turned back, but the way was passable and Cannon pressed on.

It ended in a stout fence just short of the middle of the block of housing. It looked as if some owners had been allowed to buy the area where the way had been, and include it in their back gardens. He tried to estimate where the Gyatt property would come to. There was a high, thick laurel hedge, very typical for this kind of Victorian property. If what he was hoping had any chance of being true there had to be some way in from this back path.

He pushed aside sprawling strands of laurel, looked down and reminded himself that Hoskins would think him a fool for doubting. The ground here was almost as scuffed as the entrance, padded down where someone had shuffled sideways, squeezing close between boarded fence and laurel hedge to make a way in – or out. He emerged at the back of an herbaceous border of tall ornamental evergreens.

If this newly trusted sixth – or was it seventh – sense was right then this had to be Gyatt's home. One thing was immediately obvious: it was a very private, secret garden. Large trees shielded it from any overlooking neighbouring windows, and all the hedges and ornamental borders were far too high for anyone to look over without a ladder.

He saw that soil from the border had marked the grass over to a crazy-paved path – but was he in Gyatt's garden? There was a fairly stout group of old lilacs to the side he believed to be The Rowans. If he could just glimpse Joan Burnham's garden he could be sure he was right.

His heart had begun to pound like a boy on a scrumping expedition as he carefully lodged his feet into the thickest angles of the lilacs. They swayed alarmingly but three footholds up he carefully raised his head above the bushes. Yes. Joan Burnham's garden, the view he had seen from her French windows, plus a line of washing. Silently he lowered himself to the ground and went on towards Gyatt's back kitchen window.

If there was an active alarm system his time would be limited, limited to how quickly anyone took any notice of the wail – but in that respect he was fighting the odds with an alert neighbour like Joan Burnham, and a surveillance unit at the end of the street.

He pulled a pair of gloves from his pocket and a roll of tape. He criss-crossed the small pane next to the kitchen window catch with the tape, then gave it a hefty blow with the side of his fist. It broke; just one fragment of glass tinkled into the sink. He waited – nothing. He lifted the internal catch, pulled the outward opening window as far as the bottom bar would allow, then slid his hand through. He paused again before lifting the old-fashioned stay, letting the window swing wide.

In seconds he was in, head first over the sink, sideways over the draining board, pulled his feet through, and was standing in the middle of a tiled, modernized kitchen – not half so cosy as the one next door.

All was still quiet, but the kitchen door was closed. Often house alarms operated only when a door was opened. He went on – nothing – but listening intently, wondering if Gyatt was doing the same – listening, hiding, waiting to pounce. Cat and mouse. Cannon could hardly wait to grapple with him.

The house layout was exactly like next door, but the furniture was incongruous. The straight spare lines and undecorated pale woods of the late sixties were ill at ease in the more lavish proportions of the Victorian house, Cannon decided, as he quickly looked into all the downstairs rooms.

He was becoming desperate for some lead, some evidence – something, anything – as he ran up the thickly carpeted stairs. Four doors on to the landing stood open – four en-suite bedrooms, all empty – leaving just the room that would be at the front of the house. This door had a lock and the appearance of a strong external door. He expected it to be fastened – hoped it would be – but before he pounded on it, hoping for some faint but recognizable voice to answer, he tried the handle. It gave and though he had to use some extra force to push this heavy door, it was not locked.

This room had an entirely different feel, like a bed-sitting room – but a reinforced bed-sitting room – and there was another door. This was a bathroom also empty. So he was alone in this house. This was where he had convinced himself, him and his instincts – and Hoskins' theories – that Liz had been taken by Gyatt and kept imprisoned in his mother's former quarters.

There was no doubt these rooms had been prepared with the precise object of keeping someone restrained and safe from harming themselves. These windows had internal triple glazing, with net curtains at the glass plus a projecting cage of bars and mesh, so that whoever was inside could certainly look out, but had no chance of being able to break or tap the glass, unless they had a stick, or even a chair – but there was no chair. There was a bed, and two couches but no small table – in fact no small furniture of any kind. There was a comfortable spiteful cleverness about this suite. There were some books, but there was no television, no radio. He looked back in the bathroom – here there was soap and paper towels.

He went back to stand at the window. In the fast fading-light he could see the front drive, and next door's front drive; in fact he could see Joan Burnham walking a woman to a parked car, waving her off. If Liz had been confined in this room she would have seen him come – and go. And that had been how it felt – it had felt just as Hoskins had described it – that someone was looking at him from a distance. He remembered gazing up at these windows as he left. He remembered his reluctance to leave the area, at the intense feeling he had of being in the wrong as he drove away. So had Liz been here? Had she been kept here and taken away again? 'Never doubt your instincts': another of Hoskins' oft-repeated sayings.

He swept round on the room, challenging – if she had been here he would know, wouldn't he? Wouldn't there be some sign? Wouldn't she have tried to leave some clue? But where? With what? How?

There was no writing material he could see, no tools, no cosmetics in the bathroom. All there was in the way of passing time was the tumbled pile of books on one of the couches, old-looking books like someone's great-grandfather's Sunday School prizes. But if that's all one had to do all day they could be regarded as a blessing. He went to sit by the pile and, still with his gloves on, he took up each one. *Coral Island* by R M Ballantyne, *The World's Thousand Best Poems*, a St James Bible. There had to be the complete works of Shakespeare, he thought, like on *Desert Island Discs*. There was, plus several *Golden Treasuries of Verse*.

He took them up one by one, looked at each, and piled them neatly the other side of where he sat. At the bottom of the pile, completely hidden until he had stacked the others, was the complete works of Alfred, Lord Tennyson, with one difference: this had a piece of paper sticking out, like a bookmark. A piece of paper towel from the bathroom had been folded to a neat, sharp point.

The marker kept the place at 'The Charge Of The Light

Brigade'. 'Cannon to right of them, cannon to left of them'; the familiar words came to his mind even as he made to flip the pages over, and even before his gaze fell on the third verse of the poem where the first three lines all began with the word 'Cannon'. 'Cannon to right of them, Cannon to left of them, Cannon in front of them' – and each time the word had been underscored as if with a fingernail. It was as if he heard a growing appeal: Cannon! Cannon! Cannon!

Liz had been here. He took the book to the window. If she had underscored one word, then perhaps there could be others – a message!

He angled the book to the light and could clearly see minute indentations under individual letters and words in the next verse of the same poem: 'pl' in the word 'plunged', then an 'a' in 'battery-smoke', and the 'n' and 'e' in 'line'. Plane. In the next verse the individual letters s - c - o - t, then the next verse an 'l' plus 'and' was underscored. Scotland. Plane Scotland. Was Gyatt taking Liz to Scotland?

Before he began to think how this would be possible, he punched in Austin's number on his phone. When he answered he raised his voice to drown out anything Austin was trying to say, to tell him where he was and what he had found. And whatever Austin thought of his actions, he responded to the new facts immediately. 'A private hire plane then,' he guessed.

'I would think.' But as Cannon spoke he was glancing down over the next poem in the volume. 'The Brook', it was called, 'an idyl'.

'Leave it to me,' Austin was saying as Cannon realized that the 'I' in the first line was underscored – then an 'l', an 'o' and on through the first few lines, to read 'I love you'.

'For God's sake,' he muttered and without thinking closed his phone. She had taken time to put that when she could have given more information, or – or – something. Or was it the kind of thing one did because you thought it was final, a last, message? He let out a cry that was half agony and half fury. The sound seemed to fold back on itself, going nowhere, and he knew it was not the first cry that had been uttered unheard in this room.

CHAPTER 23

AUSTIN CALCULATED THAT probably the only way there was to take a reluctant passenger on a plane was by private hire, and even that would take some doing – some plausible story, some gift of the gab, and money – but Gyatt had all those.

'The photographers have finished. The doctor's sure it was strangulation, time complicated by the heat of that furnace room, but he'll let us have a full report tomorrow.' Inspector Helen Moore relayed all that information as she walked into the farm kitchen to join Austin, and before she realized he had other things on his mind.

'Local airports,' he began, then added, 'John Cannon is in Gyatt's house.'

Her attention became more intensely focused as he went on. To her credit, he thought, was her silence; no interjections of official anger. When he'd finished she sat down at the table and tapped urgently on it as if to summon her faculties into the kind of overdrive the situation required.

'So we're assuming Cannon's partner is still alive and Gyatt's trying to get her out of the area,' she said, adding, 'There are plenty of airfields in Lincolnshire, some belonging to the air ministry, some privately owned. Though Northmarket would be both the nearest, and the one most used to handling private charter flights. In fact there's been racing there today so I guess they've been busy, wealthy owners coming in by private jets. There's a row of small private hangars, I do know that.'

'We've no way of knowing how far ahead he's planned all this,' Austin said, 'but my gut feeling is not long. Would it be possible to hire a plane at short notice?'

She shrugged. 'Money opens most doors quickly.'

'I don't what to panic Gyatt. We have an explosive situation, an outstandingly clever man turned murderer, a female hostage.'

'And she has a male partner who's your friend, who is also ex-Met – and acting outside the law.'

'Yes.' There was nothing else he could add to that and for the moment she said no more.

'Time is going to be of the essence,' he added. 'We know Gyatt was only just in front of Cannon when he was here, but in case we miss him at the airport this end we should set up a check on all flights going into Scotland's airports, large, small, private – from now.'

'I'll see to that,' she said, 'and I'll find out what the chartering situation is, and if anyone knows of anything leaving for Scotland tonight.'

'I think I'll go straight to Northmarket, mingle, see what I can see, what I can pick up.'

'And Cannon?' she asked.

'I think we have to just let him go on and do what he must.'

'And if he turns up at Northmarket airport with, say, a gun?'

He stopped at the door. 'He'd only shoot Gyatt,' he told her without looking back. 'He's still too much policeman to risk any member of the public.'

Cannon would have left Gyatt's house the way he had come, the easier to reach his car in the town, but as he set foot on the crazy-paved garden path a woman's voice called. He stopped, spun round, saw a tall, slim figure stooping under overhanging branches, hurrying towards him, and breathed her name. 'Liz?'

'Inspector?'

Joan Burnham walked nearer, more confident now she recognized him. 'I thought I heard someone. I'd stopped to break off a few dead flower stalks after seeing a friend off …' She was close enough now to see his face, and automatically caught his arm. 'Are you all right?' she asked. 'No, clearly you're not.' She glanced apprehensively back at the Gyatt home. 'No one's here, are they?'

He shook his head.

'You've had some sort of shock though,' she said. 'Come with me.'

'I need to access an online computer,' he explained. 'I need information about local airports.'

'I'm online,' she told him, and led the way briskly out of the front gate and round into her home. She led him to her computer in a corner of her dining room.

He talked as he took over the machine, requesting airports and private hire facilities. He told her of Gyatt's mother, of her removal from the private asylum as the pages loaded, turned to tell her more gently of her death – her murder. 'I don't think there's any doubt that her son—'

'I'm sure there's not,' she interrupted, her voice sharp with regret. 'One crime leads to another, doesn't it?'

And one murder to another, Cannon thought. Once the taboo of taking life had been broken it had to be easier the next time – and the next.

'Though I never thought Gerald would turn murderer.' She hesitated, then added, 'but I do understand one thing …'

'And that is?' he prompted.

'He's finally found a way to deal with his mother. All his life she's been an insoluble problem to him, a burden. Now she's finally, finally gone – and I guess he'll have to pay the price.'

'He will,' he said and heard satisfaction in his own voice.

'But the crime of his father being driven to suicide, and that was a crime I witnessed, that will go …' She paused. 'No, perhaps you could say Gerald has revenged his father.'

He did not answer, more interested in the immediate future than arguing over the irrevocable past.

'I saw him grow from a mentally tortured boy to ...' She was trying very hard to stay calm, but her voice shook. 'You've no idea the traumas I went through with him.'

'And you don't know my story,' he said quietly. 'He has a hostage, my partner, Liz.'

'A hostage?' She gasped, frowning, unable to grasp the idea. 'A hostage, when he's free of his mother? Why? Does he hope to escape, using your partner ...' Then looking down at Cannon, her lips parted in concern, her sympathies transferred. She put an arm across his shoulders. 'My dear boy.'

'No, no, please don't.' He raised his hands, alarmed by the notion of this woman, this particular woman, making a caring gesture towards him. He felt he might just turn his head into her bosom and sob like a child.

She drew back her hand and stepped away.

'Just don't be kind to me, not at this moment. I couldn't deal with it.'

A mug of coffee was placed at his elbow just as he had brought up an online service that had him half rising from the chair. It read:

Air Ambulance – Mediflight – 24 hours every day
Every care for the injured or unwell
Bed-to-bed service for long-term invalids
Being bed-bound does not mean being housebound
Long- or short-haul flights.

There was a lot more detail, plus a picture of a simple bed secured beneath a row of portholes – a bed with sets of safety straps to go over a patient's shoulders, chest, middle and legs. There was a folded blanket, blue and green plaid, on the bed, ready to cover the occupant.

'What are you thinking?' she asked.

'An unwilling traveller could be drugged and taken as an invalid – and Mediflight have a base at Northmarket.'

'I know Northmarket airport really well. I worked there after I lost my husband. I could take you a quick way via a service road that avoids all the race traffic. The roads will be chock-a-block for hours after a race meetings like today's.'

She drove him in her bright blue Ford Focus, passed the surveillance team who no doubt noted their passing, and if they were really smart also knew who he was. After clearing the suburbs she drove quickly and efficiently away from the main roads, turning in what he would have thought was entirely the wrong direction for the airport.

The final turn of the journey took them along a road between high hawthorn hedges, some well in leaf in this sheltered lane. He was doubting it was much more than a dirt track until they met a large frozen-food lorry bearing the legend 'Creative Catering', and realized this was the kind of service road that served motorway facilities. This would lead to the back of restaurants and to shop delivery points. He was wondering about security when she pulled up in a sparse dirt patch of open ground in front of high-wire boundary fences and gates, though these were open.

'We have to walk from here, but it's not far.'

Only a few yards further on she led him around the arm of an automatic barrier, and in minutes they were in front of the main terminal. 'The private hangars are over on the far side,' she told him. 'You can see them from inside, but you can't go out that way.'

It was as she gestured to the numbered passenger gates at the far side of the terminal that he saw Austin standing at a small desk to the side of the check-ins. Above Austin's head was a red illuminated sign which had small red crosses decorating all four corners and from time to time it flashed the message: 'Mediflight.'

He took the computer printout of their facilities from his pocket. If he knew Austin had these he could go off on a more unorthodox search. He turned to Joan Burnham. 'You say the private hangars are over to our right from here?' he asked.

'You can see them from the end of the building.' She made as if to walk that way.

'No, I wonder if I could ask you to do something else for me.' He was assessing her appearance as he spoke. 'Just in case Gyatt is around, would you put the scarf you have around your neck over your head, and could you walk with less of a stride....'

'Disguise myself, you mean?'

He nodded. 'I wouldn't want Gyatt to recognize you. But do you see Chief Inspector Austin over there? Would you take this to him and just tell him Cannon is looking into the private hangars.' He handed her the printout.

Austin turned, frowning, surprised to be tapped on the arm, then controlled whatever other emotion he was feeling as he recognized her, received the message and the printout.

'Thanks,' he said and folded it in two as the young uniformed woman with a hairdo like a Victorian housekeeper put down a telephone and addressed him.

'Sorry, sir, there is no one available, with the races ...'

'And flights to Scotland?'

'We are of course not at liberty to disclose ...'

'No one flying to Scotland with a sick passenger, bedridden in fact?' He rapped the question at her.

'Whatever,' she said with a shrug, but before she could say more he pushed his warrant card under her nose.

'I'm CID and a woman's life depends on this information. Have you a bedridden patient being flown out?'

She made to reach for the telephone again, but stopped as he repeated, 'A sick woman? Yes or no?'

'A husband is flying his bedridden wife to Scotland,' she said, 'but she's been sick for years and years ...'

Austin glared and leaned forward.

She blinked and added, 'He said.'

'Right, which hangar? When should it leave?'

She consulted papers, then started as his hand flattened them to her desk. 'Which hangar?' he asked again.

'Number four,' she said. 'Number four.' But Austin was already on his way.

'Get on to your flight control and stop the flight,' he ordered, 'and tell the police on duty here.'

Cannon had seen that the only way he was going to get into the private hangars was literally through some back door. There was too much activity, two many yellow-coated mechanics and men with controlling bats out front.

He ran to the back of the hangars and was immediately confronted by a stocky man in a black donkey jacket with leather patches on the shoulders. The man spread his arms. 'Whoa up, chap, what's the hurry? Public are not allowed in this area.'

'I've urgent medication for the Mediflight leaving for Scotland.' He pushed his hand into his pocket and brought out the bottle of pills Dr Purdy had brought him from the hospital. 'I'm told it's a matter of life or death, mate.'

The man assessed him. 'Hangar four,' he said, 'but you'd better hurry. I saw the medic car come some time ago.'

He pointed the way towards the front of the hangars. Cannon made as if to go that way, but once the man was out of sight he turned back. A bottle of tablets with his own name on was not going to get him far. He reached the back of the hangar, saw there was a small door, opened it and slipped inside. The hangar contained two small private jets, with space for at least two more. Neither of the remaining planes were being prepared for flight as far as he could see, though stooping he could see there were several men in overalls on the far side of the fuselages. Then another man came, from the front, through the main hangar doors which were concertinaed right back, calling to his mates, making his way over to them.

Cannon knew he would be seen any second, and began to run towards the tarmac. Immediately the man shouted. A confusion of questioning, then alarmed and angry shouts broke out behind him, plus the sound of men pounding after him.

Once outside he saw the ambulance car parked some little distance away. He was far fitter, leaner, swifter than the others and reached the Mediflight vehicle before the driver was aware anything was amiss. He was listening to a Beatles recording, a beatific smile on his face, and scanning a newspaper.

'Police!' Cannon proclaimed. 'Where's your patient?'

'On the plane,' the startled man answered, pointing to where a small plane was taxiing towards the end of a runway. 'I have to wait here until it's actually took off – company regulations.'

Cannon ignored his added, 'Why what's up?' and with no other option ran on.

Austin had commandeered one of the small tractors used to go to and from the planes, but the driver swinging round to make for the small private plane became cut off from it by a whole caravan of luggage going out to a larger jet.

He could see men running from several directions. He recognized the security police from the airport and several men in overalls lagging a long way behind a man who was sprinting towards the private plane, which was even now turning to poise on the end of a runway ready for take-off. The man looked determined to hang on to its wheels should all else fail. Cannon.

'I need to contact the control tower,' Austin told his driver. 'That plane must be stopped.' He wondered if the girl on the desk had even attempted to follow his orders. The driver dug into his breast pocket, brought out a radio-phone, pressed a button, then handed it to Austin with a nod.

'The Mediflight plane you have on the end of runway ...'

'One North,' the driver supplied.

'One North, must be stopped.'

'We know,' a grim voice replied, 'but the pilot has a gun to his head.'

So had Gyatt already seen the furore behind the plane, or was the gun to force the pilot to divert to a different destination? If it took off they might really lose him and Liz Makepeace. 'Stall them as long as you can. Say there's an obstruction on the runway, anything,' Austin ordered, his eyes on Cannon's diminishing figure, as still the load of luggage rumbled between them and the way they wanted to go. Then he saw another option.

'Quick.' He dropped a hand on his startled driver's shoulder. 'Take me up alongside that luggage tractor.'

As they approached at speed, the other driver and his companion waved them away. 'What the hell are you doing? This is not the bloody races!'

'Get in front, stop them,' Austin said as he jumped down from the moving vehicle, regaining his balance with difficulty but managing at the same time to flourish his warrant card. 'Police. We've a hostage situation – a young woman.' He pointed to the Mediflight plane. 'I'm commandeering your tractor.'

'What ...' the driver began, then realized. 'I'll drive,' he volunteered.

'He's armed.'

'Com' on, you've got kids – he gets paid for it.' His mate jerked his head in Austin's direction as he jumped down.

'Wise man,' Austin said as he pushed the vehicle as fast as its load would allow across the divide between the huge passenger jet and the tiny Mediflight plane. As he pulled across the front of the small plane, he clearly saw the pilot with Gyatt standing over him in the cockpit, the distance short, and the only barrier between them a windscreen. Their eyes met for a couple of seconds, each man alert to the other's intentions; it felt a curious knowing intimacy.

Austin saw a movement of Gyatt's hand and dived from the driving seat to conceal himself behind the luggage trolleys. Would

Gyatt risk shooting through the plane's windscreen? Would he risk taking his gun from the pilot's head? And where was Cannon?

Cannon had raised both fists in appreciation as he saw the barrier of luggage cut off the plane's flight path. Not that anyone was safe. If he was right and Liz was aboard, she could be in greater peril – and what state was she in? – and could he be this close without being able to help her?

He knew the steps to these planes were an integral part of their structure, but had the door some kind of safety feature which secured it from inside when in flight, or about to take off? He just didn't know.

He stooped under the fuselage, obscured from those who ran after him, and pulled out his gun. He took a moment to steady his breathing, or his aim would be all over the place. For a second he thought he really was off-balance, the effect of running, the giddy sensation of solid objects seeming to move, but then he realized it was the plane. It was very, very slowly beginning to reverse.

As he hurled himself out of the way the door crashed violently open, the steps and a man spewed out followed by shots from inside the plane, which came to a halt.

He registered that the man sprawling, winded, on the tarmac, wore the three-quarter-length green overall often used by medical attendants.

He lunged forward, grabbed the man by the arm and dragged him unceremoniously out of line of fire from the doorway. 'Is there a young woman patient?' he demanded in a fierce whisper.

The man gasped for air, nodded.

'Is she...?'

'Not good,' he said, recovering his breath. 'Then when the control tower told us we can't go, her husband pulls a gun.'

'Husband?'

'So he says.'

'Stay here undercover.' He patted the man on the shoulder.

'There's others coming.' Though it sounded as if the chase was being more circumspect now shots had been heard.

He moved towards the door, sidled around until he was half lying, half crouching, on the small set of steps up into the plane. Above the engine he could hear two men, or was it three? There was argument, some pleading – some distraction – and now was his time.

What he had not expected was to be unseen. His mind registered the whole interior, made a lasting photographic memory of the situation in one click of some internal lens. The bed to the side, the plaid blanket unfolded, over a form secured by the straps like a step-two illustration from the brochure printout. The form was as still, and as unreal, as a model. Cannon felt the ice-cold calculation of the determined predator take over as he forced his gaze to the front of the plane, to three men, two seated and one standing, all looking forward. Their attention on a movement, a man on the central luggage trolley, who appeared to have a rifle trained directly on them.

'Reverse!' Gyatt ordered the pilot. 'Back up, then take off. Now!'

The word was the trigger to Cannon. From experience he knew these situations had one moment in which action could succeed. This was it. He sprang on his prey. Gyatt turned as the shadow of Cannon's body arrived like warning thunder before a lightning strike. He knocked not just the gun from Gyatt's hand but the man himself in a crashing thud to the floor. Gyatt cried out in exasperation, then pain, as first his side, then his head, struck a solid metal table, displacing charts.

Cannon immediately thrust his own gun into the co-pilot's hand, picked up Gyatt's and gave it to the pilot, gestured they should both keep the fallen barrister covered – and went back to the bed.

With the tenderness of one looking at a newborn, he turned the blanket from the face, and for the first time was certain it was Liz

– but was sure of nothing else. He bent to put his cheek next to hers and found it cold. He pushed his finger into her neck. There was no warmth, nothing. Disbelieving, he moved his finger up under her chin and held his own breath until, as if by willing it, he detected the faintest of pulses.

'John?' The word held a world of questioning and he looked up into Austin's concerned face, and around at a plane overloaded with men, police, Gyatt on his feet held between two uniformed officers.

'Austin,' he appealed, 'she's alive but ...'

The medical attendant came pushing through to them. 'She's drugged, sedated, but God knows what with, what amount? It's obvious now I know she was a hostage. You need experts ... quick ... and information.' He turned on Gyatt. 'What've you given her? You, you ...'

Gyatt was trying to resist the attempt to handcuff him.

'We'll ask him,' Austin said, 'but get him out of here first.'

'I'll request the air ambulance.' The pilot lowered himself back into his seat, switched off the engine, and began communicating with the control tower.

'Utmost urgency,' Austin prompted and watched as Cannon knelt by Liz, discarded the straps and put his arm over her, his face next to hers. He could see he was talking to her.

He turned, gestured his men off the plane to give John room and some privacy for a minute or two for this reunion of a kind. The pilot and Austin were the last to leave. He put his hand gently on John's shoulder. 'You'll hear the hospital helicopter – about fifteen minutes they said.'

Outside on the tarmac, Gerald St John Gyatt shouted at him. 'I shall conduct my own defence.'

'You do that,' Austin told him, and restrained himself from adding that he would recommend a plea of insanity.

CHAPTER 24

IT WAS HOURS before Austin was able to follow Cannon to the hospital. Gyatt had refused to make any comment about how and with what he had drugged Liz. They went through his clothing, then his luggage, and found two empty pill bottles, both prescribed for 'Mrs Geraldine Gyatt, Dadd Ward', and both dated the day he had taken his mother away from the private psychiatric hospital. Austin noted the irony of the boy named after his mother. Temazepam and Diazepam, thirty of each, plus a warning not to exceed the stated four-hourly dose. He prayed that Gyatt had used most of the tablets to subdue his mother, before using what was left on Liz.

In the airport security unit Austin confronted Gyatt with their find. Asked when and how many of the pills he had given his hostage, he shrugged, almost sneered, and said, 'All of them.'

'All of those left after you had overdosed your mother?' Austin asked quietly, having subdued an overwhelming urge to crash his fist into the man's face. 'From both bottles?'

Gyatt gave a grunt of amusement.

Austin surveyed this man who had walked the same corridors as his own revered father, whose trial, when it came, would forever besmirch those Chambers. Then with all the false, theatrical joviality he could muster, and as if he might be addressing a colleague he met in that place, he asked, 'As an educated man, old boy, how many pills would you estimate were in each bottle?'

Gyatt looked at him sharply, heard the disdain, sensed perhaps for the first time his permanent exclusion from the good and the educated. 'Some, some,' he shouted, 'bloody *some*.'

'Very erudite,' Austin said and nodding to Helen Moore added, 'Take him away. They'll no doubt transfer him to London ASAP, where he'll meet many of his old criminal and legal acquaintances. There should be some interesting reunions.' He saw hands fall on Gyatt's shoulders as with a snarl he attempted to lunge after him.

Any satisfaction was short-lived when the further information on the tablets was relayed to the hospital, where it was received with grave concern. His concern now was to be by John's side, but before he could drive himself into Norwich, he had an important call to make to Chief Inspector Don Lovett. Without preamble he said, 'We've got Gyatt.'

'Aye, we 'ave,' Don Lovett confirmed. 'His flat's like a nerve centre of solicitor and estate agency businesses. He was obviously clearing out ready to run, but there's enough evidence in the last few days' post and his computer hard drive. He's gone on dealing – buying, selling, renting – properties he acquired through money laundering years ago. He obviously did the original Race Case gang big-time.'

'No wonder he didn't want too much work from Barristers' Chambers.'

'Sense of humour too,' Lovett went on. '"Wood" the name he used for his country properties, "Street" for urban properties, and – wait for it – "Wigg" for the Solicitor. Simple but clever, no chance of him mixing up the operations he was masterminding.'

'Could have forgiven him that if he hadn't gone on to abduction and murder,' Austin said.

'People progress in every profession,' Lovett said, obviously far too pleased with the success of his operation to be brought back to earth so quickly. 'Villains climb the ladder of villainy the longer they get left to do it.'

'Yes,' Austin said, remembering the paper money Gerald Gyatt had started with as a boy. 'But our news is we've recovered Liz Makepeace.'

'Aah!' The expression of satisfaction said everything about both man and policeman. 'And...?'

He told the rest of the facts.

'You'll be wanting to get over there to Cannon. No problem, get off. Let me know how they both are.'

When Austin entered the side ward, his first thought was, thank God for enlightened people with enough common sense to break a few rules. Two single beds had been pushed side by side; on one lay Liz attached to drips and monitors. Next to her the fully clothed Cannon, looking as unconscious as his partner, lay half sprawled between one bed and the other, one hand cradling Liz's, the other clenched in an uncompromising first. Heaven help anyone who tried to part them again, Austin thought, clearing a great lump from his throat to ask, 'What have you done to him?'

'Nothing, he was just totally exhausted,' the consultant, a tiny, fiery-looking, red-haired man told him. 'We could do with siphoning the excess of drugs in her blood into him to keep him sedated until he's properly rested. I've heard of "dying in harness" but never seen a man so near to achieving it. Surely the police don't need to ...'

'He's not a policeman,' Austin interrupted, 'just devoted to his partner.'

'We came to understand that.' He nodded to the unconventional arrangement of beds. 'Done what we can.'

'So she has been overdosed?'

'Oh! Yes, very much so, criminally so,' the consultant confirmed. 'I hope whoever ...'

'He's in custody,' Austin told him.

'Good!' He nodded down at the couple. 'All we can do now is what he's doing – wait. We don't pump out stomachs these days. It's very much a question of nature taking its course.'

Austin nodded, the mention of nature making him think of Hoskins, and Paul Jefferson: he must check they'd been told. He looked down at Liz, so pale, her hair looking as if cut in one of those strange raggedy styles that seemed high fashion at the moment, so vulnerable, yet he knew she was tough. She had proved that in her police days. 'Come on, Liz,' he whispered, 'Cannon needs you.' He gently took her other hand and sat beside her for a time.

Through the night Cannon woke once, and the Irish night sister brought him sandwiches and tea. She hovered over Liz, checked the drips and monitors. 'No change?' he asked. 'Are you sure?'

'Nothing visible,' she said, 'but she's with us, thanks be to God. Is there anything else you'd be wanting?'

He shook his head. 'You have the buzzer there, and I'm around all the time.' She turned to go then looked back and smiled. 'It wouldn't hurt to talk to her.'

She left him and he glanced at the clock: 2 a.m. Wasn't this the time when life was supposed to be at its lowest ebb? He went to sit on the chair, bent low over her face. He wanted to remove the oxygen mask and feel her breath on his face. He stroked the hair from her forehead, gently tidied strands beneath the elastic strap of the mask.

'Liz,' he said, the sister's words a sacred edict, and began, in a stumbling mid-sentence, 'Those … African violets … but it feels like eternity, like purgatory, with no reprieve for good behaviour – not that I've been good – Austin wouldn't think so. The opposite, I suppose. Guess if my grandfather hadn't been an old-time copper I'd never have wanted to be one. I'd have gone the other way. Been on the other side of the fence. You know my old man wanted me to be a market trader. "Lots of ackers, boy," he used to say … instead of which I ran a mile from the old fruit and veg. Joined the force and … well …' He rested his head down on the pillow next to hers; felt the draught of the oxygen cold from the mask. 'You know the rest of that story.'

He felt now that any break in this monologue was letting her down, and racked his brains. 'I went to my grandparents for holidays. We used to go fishing. Bent pin and worm job first, then fly fishing. I hooked a few bushes and once a geezer's fancy pullover before I learned to cast a fly properly. But came the day when I caught my first trout ... a rainbow ...' Distracted by the image of that multicoloured fish coming in on his line, his mind slipped back into the sleep it had been denied for so many days and nights.

He came back to consciousness aware of the uncompleted story, and with his voice thick with sleep he continued '... and I fell in, slipped, joined the fish, then my grandfather slipped in, getting me out. When we got home ...'

'Trouble,' a muffled voice suggested.

Without lifting his head he looked across the pillow, to find Liz's eyes open, her mouth curving enough to make a smile.

'I ...' he began, hardly daring to believe, then he felt her hand holding his, gripping his, and deep in his stomach there was a throb of great tearful laughter which surfaced as a tiny, questioning, 'Liz?'

He lifted himself from the pillow. She nodded to him and through the mask said, 'Hi.'

'Hi yourself!' he said and had the ridiculous sensation that he was dreaming and it was all underwater, what with the mask and the blurry vision.

Then a door opened and Sister was in the room by his side. 'Ah! God be praised!' she said. 'I've been watching, seeing the signs, and now here you are both back in the land of the living.' She reached over to slip off the oxygen mask. 'There,' she said, 'have a love of her for a minute while I get the doctor.'

It was a phrase that was going to slip into their love language. 'Have a love of her for a minute.'

CHAPTER 25

Austin was early at Liverpool Street Station, but not as early as Don Lovett, who to his surprise walked towards him from the far end of the platform. The chief inspector looked older, and heavier, in civilian clothes, but his smile and handshake left nothing to be desired.

'Seen Parmar?'

Austin nodded, remembering how his father's old clerk had taken it all so very personally, as if it was some failure on his part that would eventually bring such terrible notoriety to his Chambers. 'My father arrived while I was there.'

'Embarrassing?' Lovett asked.

'Awkward,' Austin replied, wanting to add that his father was in any and every case the very soul of discretion, but not doing so.

'And?'

'Gyatt kept nothing to do with his criminal activities there – in fact, his desk drawers were empty.' Mahendra Parmar had stood shaking his head. 'The only thing he has in his room of interest to us is a showcase of manacles, shackles, handcuffs …'

'All the restraining devices,' Lovett murmured.

'Mr Parmar pointed out that there was a pair of fifties' police cuffs missing. They could have been the ones he used on Hoskins.'

'Right,' Lovett said as their train to Norwich drew in. 'That'll be in his statement. Parmar will undoubtedly be called as a witness.'

Austin shook his head, wishing Parmar could be kept out of the affair.

'Better than your father being involved,' Lovett turned to say as they boarded.

Once in their first-class seats, both men realized they were not going to be able to talk with any degree of freedom. Lovett gave him the slightest of nods and both rose and went through to the dining car. 'What are you serving?' he asked the middle-aged lady attendant.

'Breakfast's still on, sir, either full English or coffee and croissants.'

Lovett nodded to the empty far end of the compartment. 'Over there. Two full English and tea?' Austin nodded. 'But coffee for me, please.'

'Make yourselves comfortable, gentlemen, I'll bring your tea and coffee first.'

'You've seen Liz Makepeace?' Lovett asked even as he landed heavily in his seat, assisted by a sudden sway of the train.

He had seen her quite a few times in the last three weeks, but what he recalled was not just Liz, but Cannon, leaving the hospital together. They had walked quite slowly along the hospital corridor, both looking thinner, older, taller somehow – solemn until they caught each other's eye, then smiling, such slow, sweet smiles. Austin had found he must blink his gaze away, and for a second or two regretted his solitary state. He had arrived at the hospital with an offer from his father of the family's seaside bungalow, and his own to drive them there. Liz had looked at Cannon, shook her head and said she just wanted to go home.

'Going to weather it, are they?' Lovett asked.

'She's talking about it all,' Austin said.

'Important that.'

'In retrospect she says the worst part of all was when the shooting happened at the mill. She thought she was being rescued, and even when Gyatt came into the room where she was tied up, she thought he was a plain-clothes man. She said she knelt up on her sleeping bag, smiling, thanking him, holding up her hands to be cut loose.'

'Christ,' Lovett breathed, then raised a warning hand as he saw the attendant coming back with their drinks.

'But she actually said it was Gyatt who looked shaken as she knelt there,' Austin resumed. 'She said she must have looked as if she was praying to him, hands tied together ...' He paused to stir his coffee. 'And you see there's an aspect of this case which you are unaware of.'

Lovett gently sipped and blew his tea by turns, and waited.

'Gyatt's neighbour, Joan Burnham, when young must have looked very like Liz. I think Gyatt saw it in that moment when she knelt, smiling up at him, thinking she'd been saved. When Cannon first interviewed Joan Burnham, he saw it, and was shaken by the resemblance.'

'Didn't know civilians did interviews,' Lovett said, returning his cup to its saucer.

'No, slip of the tongue,' Austin said, grinning. Nothing much escaped Lovett. 'But we are talking Cannon – and I do think that likeness saved Liz's life.'

'I've heard of people being murdered because they reminded the murderer of someone, but not of anyone being saved because they were like somebody else.'

'Redresses the balance a bit,' Austin said, sitting back ready for the ample breakfasts coming their way.

'You are sure about tonight?' Cannon asked as he and Liz stood looking over the front of their pub. He was nervous about it, if he was honest, but he had to acknowledge that The Trap was looking good. The two of them had filled all the tubs and boxes with yellow, blue and purple pansies, and for their official reopening that night fairy lights had been looped along the eaves and in the front porch.

His concern was Liz. She knew they were reopening but nothing more. Since she had been discharged from Norwich Hospital, John felt she had never been still. Even when he insisted they both put their feet up in the afternoons she'd had pad and pen in her hands making plans, devising recipes for more home-cooked bar meals. It was as if she dare not let mind or body be still.

It was only a week ago that things had reached a crisis point, like an illness that had to peak before tipping one way or another.

She had caught him watching her one afternoon as she sat in the dining area of the pub. 'You think I'm going to crack up,' she accused.

'I just wish you'd really rest,' he said mildly and going over to where she sat had tried gently to take the pad and pencil from her.

'No,' she had resisted.

'Come on,' he had said, laughing, as if it were just a game.

'No!' She was suddenly up on her feet. 'Leave me alone. I'm planning. Planning! You stupid, stupid, man, don't you realize it's what kept me sane? Planning. Planning. Planning.' Her voice was near a scream by the end.

He approached her with his arms open, wanting to contain her distress. This, or something like, was what he had feared. 'Liz, please ...'

She backed away from him. 'No, don't try to ...' She threw her arms up and away as if throwing off constraints. 'I'm dealing with this my own way.'

'Look, I know how ...'

'I feel!' she exclaimed and began striding round between the tables, then turned on him. 'No! You've no idea how I feel. No idea how it felt to see you walk away from that house, when I was locked in a room above you, unable to reach the window, to make you hear.'

'I found your message,' he said, but stayed quite still, watching, waiting until his instincts told him what to do next. 'That was clever of you.'

'Clever! It didn't feel clever. I didn't know you were going to find it, did I? I thought you were just walking away. You were all right, Jack, weren't you, Jack! All right Jack!'

He went to her then, and as she had tried to fight him off, unwind his arms from her, take his hands from her, he held her tight, silently contained her, until she sobbed in his arms. At first he let her, but as the sobbing grew and her whole body was racked with the ferocity of it, he had been fearful again, and had begun rocking and shushing her as if she were a distressed child. She had resisted, sworn at him, beat at him with her fists – but his instinct had said hold on, and he had, until the beating became clinging.

'You,' she sobbed, 'walking away. I couldn't make you hear.'

'But I sensed you were there. I went back because I sensed you were there.'

There had been one last beating of her fists as she told him, 'I saw you in that bloody mac. Why can't you ever do it up! Why can't you ...'

Then she relaxed so suddenly in his arms he thought she had fainted.

'Liz?'

'I'm ... sorry,' she had said, head on his shoulder, her voice normal, 'but I realize now that was the worst moment, watching you walk away, wondering if I was ever going to see you again.'

He had been so lost in the memory of that so recent trauma, he started as she moved from his side to tidy the odd dead leaf from the flower tubs. 'You know if you do find it all too much,' he said, 'we could still go away for a holiday, or sell up. Whatever you want.'

She turned to him and smiled. 'I wasted enough of my life last time. If I run away, I'll take the bad memories, the bad dreams with me, I know that. We both know that – and I love it here. Where else would we find so much goodwill?'

He knew that was true. As their story had become known the trickle of cards and flowers had become an avalanche. Every room in the pub was still full of flowers.

'I want to be here to thank them,' she said. 'I want to hang Paul's portrait of Hoskins in the bar, and those old prints are coming out of the dining area.' She paused to receive his shrug of consent. 'And a permanent display of Paul's work is going to hang in there. I'll get myself some little red stickers and every time I sell one for him my heart will rejoice. That's what I'd like to do.'

John nodded. He and Paul had been friends before, but these last weeks had cemented a lifelong caring relationship. 'We might boost his classes too if when we convert the stables we advertise tutored painting classes as well as birdwatching.'

'So we have to open to catch up with some of our lost takings,' she said. 'Come on, we've time for a walk before tea.'

He was a little taken by surprise. 'You've played into my hands.'

'What d'you mean?' she asked.

'I was just going to suggest the same thing.'

'There's no one's hands I'd rather be in,' she said, 'so come on, let's go.'

There was all the old challenge in her voice. Here was the Liz who drove the car through puddles, who cosseted old Hoskins, who made love to him with such attention. His heart rejoiced, while knowing that there would be bad days – and nights. 'How long do you think it'll take your hair to grow again?' he asked.

She considered his question, pushing a suddenly unsteady hand through the shaped blonde cap of hair. 'It may take some time,' she said.

'That's all right,' he said. 'I may have learnt to button my mac by then.'

She caught his hand, and humbled him completely by kissing it. 'There's not much we don't understand about each other, is there?'

They walked into the wind and towards the sea. On the earth bank overlooking East Salt Marsh they stood for a long time watching the shadows of the clouds racing across the greens, browns and blues of the land and seascape.

'The world looks endless from here,' she said, 'and full of many shining waters.'

Together, he thought, this woman and this place fill my heart. He gripped her hand tighter and they walked on, she absorbed in the wide freedom. He knew exactly what he was doing, realized how far he was taking her and exactly how the time was slipping by.

It was not until she saw the square tower of Reed St Thomas church that she realized how far they had walked. 'No wonder my legs are beginning to feel tired. We must get back, we'll be late.'

'No worry, Paul has a key. He's going to be there at opening time.'

'Yes, but we should be there.'

'Look, the Angel Tea Room's opened up for the season,' he said. 'I could do with five minutes' sit down and a cuppa.'

'We should be back to open up,' she persisted.

'Come on, let's patronize them on their first day,' he said, then remembered with a stroke of inspiration, 'They sent flowers.'

They were given quite a reception, not allowed to pay, and kept talking so long John had no more worries about arriving back at The Trap too soon.

She tutted as they reached the pub, for the fairy lights were all on and the front door open. 'There!' she exclaimed. 'Paul has beaten us to it.' She made to scurry round to the back, but John caught her arm. 'I think,' he said, 'they will want us to go in by the front door.'

She half turned to protest, then saw the look on his face. 'What's going on?' she asked, looking from him to the front porch, where the door through to the bar now swung open. Paul stood inside. 'Come in,' he said, 'we're open.'

Before Liz had time to think of anything to say, John had propelled her through the door into the bar, which from silence went to roars of cheering, greetings and cries of 'Surprise, surprise!'

She would have stepped back but John was too close behind her. 'You knew,' she turned to say, and he nodded.

'But not my idea.'

She looked round as if to find someone to blame. Her eyes went from Paul to Hoskins to Austin to ...

'C.I. Lovett,' she gasped, and stepped forward, suddenly in the swim, in the mood. She turned slowly round, seeing now the long trestle table laden with food, Jane Purdy and Buddy Brompton's wife in charge, waving, men from the darts teams, Paul's painting class. Hoskins, in his usual seat next to the bar, raised his glass to her. She made first for Paul and Austin, who stood next to Don Lovett and Helen Moore, then suddenly Dr Purdy was standing on a chair next to the bar, leading the singing.

'For they are jolly good fellows, for they are jolly good fellows ...'

Outside a 'V' of geese crossed the sky, winging towards the sea and another journey.